D1169370

DEATH WAS THE ECHO

DEATH WAS THE ECHO

Lauran Paine

**Willimantic Library
Service Center
1216 Main Street
Willimantic, CT 06226**

Chivers Press • G.K. Hall & Co.
Bath, England   Thorndike, Maine USA

This Large Print edition is published by Chivers Press, England, and by G.K. Hall & Co., USA.

Published in 2000 in the U.K. by arrangement with Robert Hale Ltd.

Published in 2000 in the U.S. by arrangement with Golden West Literary Agency.

U.K. Hardcover ISBN 0–7540–4014–3 (Chivers Large Print)
U.S. Softcover   ISBN 0–7838–8846–5 (Nightingale Series Edition)

Copyright © 1975 by Lauran Paine in the British Commonwealth
Copyright © 2000 by Lauran Paine

All rights reserved.

The text of this Large Print edition is unabridged.
Other aspects of the book may vary from the original edition.

Set in 16 pt. New Times Roman.

Printed in Great Britain on acid-free paper.

British Library Cataloguing in Publication Data available

Library of Congress Cataloging-in-Publication Data

Dana, Richard, 1916–
    Death was the echo / by Richard Dana.
       p.   (large print)   cm.
    ISBN 0–7838–8846–5 (lg. print : sc : alk. paper)
    1. Police—California—Los Angeles—Fiction.
    2. Large type books. 3. Los Angeles (Calif.)—Fiction. I. Title.
PS3566.A34 D46   2000
813'.54—dc21
                                   99–057949

CHAPTER ONE

THE AWKWARD CORPSE

The making of history seems to be a preoccupation of the few, while the great millions of people who, in the ongoing tableaux of their everlasting arrivings and departings, although immersed from first breath to last in one or another of history's epochal interludes, highs or lows, seem neither cognizant of a grand destiny, nor concerned with an ultimate glory. They seem, instead, to be born with a compulsion to survive, to fit into a mainstream of monotonous nine-to-five continuity which demands all of their efforts, their talents, and their time.

When the insistent demands of the history-creators require it, the un-history-makers climb out of their paths, descend from their mountains, turn inward from their seas, walk down from their endless and countless offices.

And make war. And prove themselves spiritually, mentally, inherently and atavistically unchanged and unchangeable from Chaldea to now.

It wasn't a bad conclusion to arrive at with one's morning coffee. It did not mean there was no hope, because, obviously, Sumeria and Chaldea were orderly civilizations two, three, four thousand years before Christ, and

1

although people then, as now, functioned the same, at least were motivated by the same impulses, and although Sumeria and Chaldea, and even the Thousand Year Reich, were no more, the *people* were still arriving and departing. In fact, they were doing so on a vaster scale, so, evidently, there was to be no end, except in the microcosmic context. And, there was a historic solution to all the abrasions, all the cruelties and barbarities: people forgot. Not, one could fairly assume, because they wanted to, especially, but because that monotonous demand upon their time and talents required it. It was not possible to make a living and keep alive old antipathies at the same time. Further, life was short; before the memories of one generation could fade, succeeding generations arrived, matured, to whom the earlier barbarities and antipathies were unknown except as figments of history, and that brought the whole thing round again, into a different perspective: who really cared that, in 1933, by Presidential Decree, the German policy of 'Schutzhaft' came into being. *Schutzhaft* being the Third Reich's system of 'protective custody', and before it ended a little more than a decade later, *schutzhaft*, under its *Schutztaffen*—SS—administrators, had accounted for the unbelievably barbaric deaths of, perhaps, eight million human beings, and this number accounted for no less than three-fourths of all the fatalities

2

perpetrated by the Germans in invaded and occupied countries.

By the year 1975 *Schutzhaft* wasn't even a common word in Germany, let alone the rest of the world. History had come and gone, as it always had, and along with it had gone all its creators and nearly all of its sustainers.

A generation is thirty years. Not long, actually, but long enough to dilute hatred and minimize recall. Once an epoch is finished, everyone has to get back to the business of making a living, of trade and commerce, of development and accumulation, of living, and of dying, and thirty years sees an awful lot of those things, but mostly of dying. Who remembered any more, and a generation later, who really cared? It had come, stamped its mark on history, and it had gone.

The eggs and toast that went with the coffee, helping to regenerate the heartbeat after a long night's sleep, encouraged all this philosophical acceptance. It also helped to dull the imagination, and in any case, Inspector Reg Forster had no idea what a production-line crematorium smelled like, or what eight million queued-up living skeletons looked like. That was history, and this was Los Angeles, California, with a golden sun shining, with people hurrying in and out of the restaurant across from Wilshire Division, so it was more than a bridgeless gap of years, it was also light-years away in perspective.

3

He hadn't even been born when the first stunned conquerors had stood in the gateway of Mauthausen, Natzweiler, Auschwitz, Belsen or Neuengamme. His only genuine interest in those places had occurred the previous Friday when the corpse subsequently identified by Records and Identification as one Harold Oberhauser, began to emerge from a thirty-year-old benign obscurity to become something quite different from what the routine check of Oberhauser Industries had indicated.

Even now, as Inspector Forster paid his tab and ambled across the street to his office—shared with John Blaine, another homicide detective—what he had read last evening before going home, was more like a fantasy than anything real. But what made it difficult to co-relate was Harold Oberhauser's role as an SS officer, then, and his life-style as a wealthy manufacturer, since then. Oberhauser Industries had a very enlightened and sympathetic history as a leader among manufacturers for its labour policies, for its advocacy of the four-day work-week, for its pension scheme, hospitalization, and broadly-based fringe benefits. They had all come down from the executive suite of majority-shareholder, President and Chairman of the Board, Harold Oberhauser, himself, and that, in Reg Forster's mind, made it seem improbable that his murderer could possibly have come out of the dim, brutal past of this man who had been honoured by liberals, educators, sociologists, and government officials over the past quarter century for his undisputed humanitarianism.

When he entered the office John Blaine looked up from the stapled folio pages he was reading and said, 'You've got a beauty this time,' and slapped the papers. 'It's like two different people. Oberhauser the SS captain, and Harold Oberhauser the industrialist who has made a name for himself as a defender of the common slob.' Blaine leaned to place the report carefully upon the desktop. 'When I was a kid I had an uncle who was at Omaha Beach, and from there right on through to Berlin, and in the mopping up afterwards. I've heard him tell my father some of the things he saw at those concentration camps. It'd make your hair stand straight up.'

Forster went to his desk, sat down, glanced at his mail baskets, which were empty, then turned his square, tanned face with its rock-steady grey eyes towards John Blaine. 'I read up on that subject last night. You have any idea how many people were killed in those places? Eight million. That'd be like taking a third of the entire population of California into custody, then shooting, burning, cremating, and beating them all to death.'

Blaine fished inside his jacket for a cigar and lit it. 'Hard to grasp,' he mumbled, around the cigar.

Forster grunted, then swivelled round to shove open the window at his back. John smoked awful cigars. As he swung back he said, 'That's not my point. That was done and nothing can undo it. I'm not minimizing it at all. What I'm thinking about is this: eight million people had vengeful relatives. Most people have at least two or three relatives— some have as many as ten or twenty relatives. Multiply eight by the least figure, two or three, and you come up with one hell of a lot of suspects. Sixteen to twenty-four million of them. That's my point, John.'

Blaine's retort was quick and practical. 'Oberhauser was stationed at Neuengamme. You'll only have to concentrate on the people put to death at that one camp—probably. Also, as Captain Hastings said yesterday afternoon, when all this other stuff turned up on Oberhauser, maybe it created a smoke screen, very likely whoever killed him had nothing at all to do with his earlier life. They just hated his guts because he was a rich industrialist, or maybe because there was a fancied injustice.'

Forster said, 'Hell; that doesn't *lessen* the odds, John, that *increases* them. Now, we're going to be looking for a nut who could have been a son or even a grandson of some poor devil shot or hanged in a German torture camp, out of perhaps as many as a million such descendants, or we're going to be looking for someone over here, in the US, who hated

6

Sturmbannfuhrer Oberhauser for some other motive, possibly one having to do with the more commonplace and modern reasons for killing a rich industrialist—like envy.'

John leaned to study the first page of the report in front of him, cigar smoke rising fragrantly round his heavy, good-natured face. He straightened back with a shrug and said, 'What's a *Sturmbannfuhrer?*'

'Major,' grunted Reg Forster, digging in his desk for a small, worn book which he spread upon the desktop, opened to a marked page, and read aloud: 'Neuengamme: Ninety to a hundred thousand prisoners passed through the Neuengamme network of camps of which between forty and fifty thousand were either starved to death or murdered, that is, shot to death, hanged, or bludgeoned to death, without any kind of a trial.' Reg looked up. 'Oberhauser was on duty at Neuengamme for two full years.' He closed the book and put it back in the desk-drawer. 'It doesn't square, John; how does a a man shoot people in the back of the head for two years, then come over here, take out citizenship papers, and become a model citizen, for the next twenty-five or thirty years.'

Blaine groped for an answer, and came up with one. 'He was a soldier. He obeyed orders.'

Forster's tough, grey eyes steadied upon his associate. 'Oh for Christ'sake,' he exclaimed, in great disgust.

7

Blaine made an expansive gesture. 'That's what I remember reading from their trials. Those officers said they were simply obeying orders.'

Forster arose to go stand at the window looking down into the unattractive, macadamized parking area behind Wilshire Division. He did not even bother to dispute John Blaine's last remark. Instead, he said, 'All we've got to do, is—'

'We? That's the second time you've said that.'

Forster now turned. 'Cap said you and me. He told me that last night over the telephone after I got home. He also told me there would be hell to pay over this guy's murder. He was the idol of everyone in Los Angeles who believes in motherhood, law and order, and apple pie.'

Blaine said no more about being pulled into the assignment. It would not have done one bit of good. When Ben Hastings made an assignment, adopted a conviction, or zeroed in on a goal, all the angels in heaven in conjunction with all the imps from hell, could not budge him. Blaine dusted ash from his cigar in the huge glass ashtray atop his desk, then said, 'Which aspect of this guy's past do you want? You'd better take the war years; I can't even sneeze in German.'

Forster returned to the desk. 'We're not going to split it up, we're going to work it together, and for the time being we're not going to mention this report the FBI borrowed from the CIA on Oberhauser. We're going to act as though this is just another routine murder, which it probably is ... which it sure as hell better be, or we're going to be in trouble up to our butts; not only was Neuengamme a very popular place to liquidate people, and not only do there have to be hundreds of thousands of descendants wandering around, but all that stuff happened before you and I were born, and digging that far back, even in this country, would pose problems.'

John leaned to kill his cigar. Afterwards, he picked up the report again, got comfortable, and probably would have been quite content to spend the hot morning reading in the cool seclusion of the office, but Reg Forster arose and said, 'Let's go.'

Blaine put down the report, sighed up to his feet, and followed without asking where they were going.

CHAPTER TWO

TWO ROUTINE VISITS

There had been a time in Los Angeles when the most desirable and exclusive residential area had been Beverly Hills, but times had

9

changed greatly over the past two or three decades, and in any case, as John Blaine commented, when he discovered they were heading out to Westwood Village to seek the Oberhauser residence, it would be difficult to imagine a former German World War Two *Sturmbannfuhrer* sleeping blissfully in an area which had become ninety-nine per cent Jewish within the past twenty years.

Westwood Village hadn't been a 'village', either, in many years. At one time it had been, and a very attractive one at that, set upon its low, rolling hills, cooled by the ocean air coming upcountry and inland from Santa Monica's Pacific beaches, but the expansion of Los Angeles had absorbed Westwood Village exactly as it had absorbed dozens of other serene little drowsy villages from former times.

Still, Westwood hadn't suffered the same degeneration which seemed, in Southern California at least, to follow the Israelization of a community. Furthermore, Westwood, at least the part of it Forster and Blaine visited, just south of the truly exclusive enclave of Bel-Air, was by and large an area where householders had originally been allotted larger plots of ground, so the impression of clotted closeness did not exist. The Oberhauser residence, in fact, had a very respectably large front and rear garden. So large, in fact, that they required the services of a gardener who came round twice a week.

10

The house, too, like the grounds, was so perfectly a part of its surroundings, blended so delightfully with the roses, the trees, the flowering shrubs, that until one was standing upon the very long, cool patio, with its flooring of old hand-made brick, one did not really appreciate that this, in fact, was actually a very large, commodious, and very expensive, residence.

The maid who opened the door had rosy cheeks, light grey, laughing Irish eyes, and a smile that could charm a bird right down out of his tree. Inspector Forster showed his identification folder, John Blaine did the same, and the maid said Mrs Oberhauser could not see anyone, that she was presently in her suite, under sedation, and that her doctor was with her.

Forster would have settled for a discussion with the maid, but a bull-necked, weathered man of medium height and almost grotesque thickness, appeared without a sound around the side of the house and stood down at the lower end of the patio, listening and unsmiling. When the maid saw this squat, massive man, she started closing the door as she said, 'I'm sorry. Mrs Oberhauser can see no one. Perhaps, if you called later . . . ?' The door closed silently but firmly.

Both detectives turned to gaze at the unmoving, thick man, and both of them picked up the same projected wavelengths of wary, bleak, fearless hostility. They strolled down to the massive man. Forster showed his identification folder for the second time, and introduced John Blaine, then tried a smile.

The thick man did not smile in return, but he acknowledged the presence of the law by saying, 'Good morning, gentlemen. My name is Joseph Kramer. I am Mr Oberhauser's chauffeur.' Kramer shrugged massive shoulders. 'I also do other things.' He looked steadily at Reg Forster, only spending one glance upon John Blaine, when they were introduced. Joseph Kramer seemed to be one of those individuals who unerringly picked out someone in charge, and concentrated fully upon this one man. It was not an uncommon characteristic, except that this time, Forster had the feeling that he was being mentally pinched and prodded before being popped into a witch's kettle. Joseph Kramer's dark eyebrows met above his nose, running in an uninterrupted line from one side of his face to the other side. His mouth, while long, lacked lips, and his eyes were close-spaced, unblinking, almost serpent-like in their intensity.

It might have helped if he smiled, but he did not do so, not even when John Blaine turned on his charm, which was considerable because John Blaine, a very large and powerful man, had always been able to afford to be charming, even to people he knew were dangerous.

12

Kramer said, 'I remember you with the others, Inspector Forster, when the police arrived after the killing.' The corded, powerful body slumped slightly. 'I can tell you nothing more now, except that Mrs Oberhauser is inside with the doctor, and can't see anyone at present.'

Forster nodded. 'So the maid said.' He gazed steadily at the thicker and older man. 'What we would like to know, Mr Kramer, is if anyone in the family, or anyone who works here at the house, could name anyone who was hostile to Mr Oberhauser; a neighbour, for example, a social acquaintance, a business associate.'

Kramer slowly shook his head. 'No one, Inspector. Not a single person that I know of. Mr Oberhauser was a highly respected man. The people at his factory were loyal to him. There were labour troubles elsewhere, but never at Oberhauser Industries. You should go down there and question the people. Here, at the residence, there could be no one, either.' Kramer glanced around, over at the wrought-iron, white-painted garden furniture where Harold Oberhauser had been sitting, reading, when the gunshot had ended his life. Kramer's intent, bright and expressionless eyes remained fixed over there. 'I can't understand it.' He raised a thick arm to point. 'You see; there is a brick wall behind those shrubs. It is hidden by them in fact, because Mr

Oberhauser did not like walls, did not like to feel closed in. Well; your men searched and found no place where the assassin had stood, or crouched.' The thick arm dropped back to Kramer's side, the intent, greyish eyes came back to Forster's face. 'I am baffled. He had no enemies.'

John Blaine dryly said, 'Yeah. He had *one,*' and Joseph Kramer flicked a cold look at Blaine, then looked steadily at Reg Forster again.

'Allow Mrs Oberhauser two or three days, Inspector. I'm sure she won't be able to help you any more than I can, or the maid, or anyone else, but if you'll give her time to recover a little . . .'

Forster agreed. 'That's what we'll do. Thanks for your co-operation, Mr Kramer.' He turned and led the way back to the unmarked, dark department car, slid behind the steering wheel, and wordlessly drove back out upon Sunset Boulevard, this time heading for the pass through the hills which would take them over into the San Franando Valley, and out through what had once been a beautiful farming area, and which was now a great, untidy urban sprawl, to the industrial community at the town of Burbank, where Oberhauser Industries was located. Forster spoke only when John Blaine said, 'I'll tell you something; that guy back there reminds me of some kind of neanderthal man. His build, his

14

bullet-head, those rattlesnake eyes, and the way he talks, slowly, like he's chewing each individual word.'

Forster's retort was the result of analytical thought, the result of his silence up to now. 'He's managed to just about stifle some kind of accent, which is why he talks like that, slow, careful, concentrating on enunciation.'

Blaine said, 'German?'

Forster nodded. 'I'd say so. When we get back run him through the ID system, John.'

Blaine agreed to do this, then he said, 'If he's a kraut, and Oberhauser was a—'

'Yeah, I know,' muttered Forster, interrupting. 'That's what's been in my mind too, and I don't like the implications one damned bit. If Kramer knew Oberhauser back during the war in Germany, we stand a very good chance of being pushed back twenty-five or thirty years into that mess, which is exactly what I've been hoping very hard wouldn't happen.'

Oberhauser Industries was a series of buildings, one quite large, very modern, cement, glass and steel administration structure, and, scattered elsewhere over a five acre, macadamized area, other larger, less presentable, factory-type buildings. Forster knew, from his initial research, that Oberhauser Industries manufactured aircraft components, along with a rather extensive sideline of parts for trucks, buses and boats.

15

He also knew who to contact, an individual named Ray Johnson who was Harold Oberhauser's liaison man, his dog-robber, but whose official capacity sounded a lot better: General Manager in Charge of Production. When he and John Blaine finally found Ray Johnson, he was not in his elegant office in the Administration building, he was over in the Engineering Department, across two acres of unyielding blacktop paving, and as a result of the swift communications system of Oberhauser Industries, when the pair of large detectives got over there, Ray Johnson was waiting just inside a small, air-conditioned entrance-way, where a very attractive red-headed woman seemed to do double duty as an impromptu receptionist, and a stenographer for someone at Engineering.

Ray Johnson was a youngish, crop-haired, blue-eyed man with a charming smile, a firm handclasp, and a slightly predatory look. He led the detectives into a small cubicle of an office, containing an empty desk, several chairs, and one small window, which put John Blaine in mind of the oldtime interrogation cubicles they'd used in LAPD when he'd first hired on.

Johnson's friendly look had a probing toughness behind it, but Reg Forster liked Johnson. He was the kind of a man most other efficient, no-nonsense men would like. At least at first impression. How well he would 'wear' only time could tell.

Reg put the same questions to Johnson he had put to Joseph Kramer, and got roughly the same answers, but with less stolidity, more good-natured tolerance, and better grammar, but it all amounted to the same thing: why anyone would want to kill Mr Oberhauser was a mystery. A very deep and abiding mystery. According to Ray Johnson, who said he'd worked for Mr Oberhauser seven years, since graduation from the University of Southern California—with a major, and a degree, in business administration—Harold Oberhauser did not have an enemy in the world.

Forster and Blaine impassively gazed from Ray Johnson to one another, and back to Johnson again. In the *world* was the wrong word; it made them want to flinch. Forster had a question.

'Before Mr Oberhauser organized his company, Mr Johnson, do you know what he did for a living, and where he lived?'

Johnson considered, then smiled disarmingly. 'I'm not sure, but I think I heard some years back that he ran a factory in New York. Something like that. I *do* know that when anyone was tactless enough to pry, Mr Oberhauser would pat them on the back and say that it didn't matter much what a man's origin was; if he sincerely wanted to get ahead, he should concentrate on working. He told me more than once that virtue, brilliance, and all

17

the rest of it were not worth as much as persistence. Work, and work hard, and don't be diverted from working, and you'll reach the top eventually.' Johnson smiled at Reg Forster. 'It's good advice, and coming from a man who went out of his way to help others get up there, it was worth a lot.'

'Yeah,' said Forster dryly. 'Give your best to whatever you're doing, and keep on giving it.'

'Exactly,' exclaimed the younger man, eyeing Forster's strong, tanned face with respect.

Forster looked around the little cubicle as he said, 'You said Harold Oberhauser did not have an enemy in the world, Mr Johnson . . .'

The younger man spread his hands over the obvious inconsistency. 'Well, he certainly had *one* enemy, didn't he, Inspector?'

Reg smiled. 'Yes, and he was a fair shot. One bullet through the heart, dead-centre. That's not the kind of an enemy a man needs. And Mr Johnson, no one gets up where Mr Oberhauser was, without stepping on toes, does he?'

Johnson, stuck with his grand eulogy, coloured slightly. 'What I meant was, I can't for the life of me imagine who would shoot him. I mean—shooting someone isn't how the game is played in industrial circles, anyway.'

'How is it played, then?'

'Well; I suppose you could say that when you want a man out, in industry, you fire him, if you can, and if that's not possible, you exert shareholding pressure. As a final resort, I suppose you would create a campaign to destroy his credibility with his customers—in our case here at the plant, with the prime contractors we sub-contract from. But Inspector—*shooting* someone, that's a Mafia sort of thing, isn't it?'

John Blaine smiled at Ray Johnson. 'Guns aren't partisan nor particular,' he said softly, and crossed to the little window to look out. The view was not very inspiring, unless a person liked to look at factories, raw-material stockpiles, and boxed freight sitting upon shipping docks.

CHAPTER THREE

A BAD DAY

When they got back to Wilshire Division, Blaine turned in three names to be put through the grinder, Joseph Kramer, Ray Johnson, and Irene Oberhauser. Then he went upstairs, where Reg Forster was in conversation with Bureau Chief Ben Hastings, one of the few Los Angeles Police Department veterans who, despite being grey, and seasoned from long years in homicide, was an understanding and sympathetic department head. He was not soft in any way, but he had done it rung by rung, and hadn't forgotten how it had been. *That* made a difference. Ben Hastings never raised his voice. He never had to. The men who worked for him knew exactly what was expected of them. They also knew from experience that the men who mistakenly put Ben Hastings down as one of those veteran policemen who, with only a few more years to go before retiring, did not provoke confrontations, awakened one fine morning to discover that they had been either demoted, or transferred. Ben Hastings seldom argued with his officers, and he even more rarely accepted an excuse, but he neither drove his men, nor sat in harsh judgement upon them. As a result, Wilshire Division's Homicide Bureau was one of the best in the country, and had been called the best in California, which was saying quite a bit, when one understood that if California had been a nation instead of one of the fifty states, in wealth, in export-import capability, even in population, it would have ranked fifth in the world!

Hastings was a burly man with a smile. Unlike Harold Oberhauser he had enemies, plenty of them, but it did not appear to bother him very much. In fact, as he and Reg Forster were saying, as John Blaine walked in, *everyone* had enemies, and in a world increasingly breeding up the *quantity* of people rather than the *quality* of them, a man's enemies had never had a better opportunity for killing him than they had nowadays; enemies had to be taken seriously.

With that philosophical gem tucked away, and while Captain Hastings was lighting a cigar, as Reg turned and raised the window, wearing a long-suffering expression as he did this, John reported that he had put three names into the ID mill, and went to sit at his desk.

Hastings, cigar firmly in place, asked which three names, and Blaine told him. Then the captain stunned both the inspectors by saying, 'Well; there's a little problem. Last night a man named Howarth got me out of bed after midnight, calling from Washington. He's with the Central Intelligence Agency. He had a copy of our teletype to the FBI in front of him, and he was disturbed. Harold Oberhauser doesn't seem to have been simply a very respectable business man.' Hastings removed the cigar, met the steady stares he was getting, and stated the rest of it in his quiet, pleasant voice.

'You've seen the preliminary file-search on Oberhauser; his connection with the German SS back during the Second World War. Howarth told me there's more to it. He said he'd be arriving out here tomorrow. He also said he would appreciate being able to work with us in this mess.'

John Blaine eased back slowly, in his chair,

21

and Reg Forster, the philosophy major who had ended up a homicide detective because he hadn't been able to find a professorship open at a college, sat forward, hands lightly clasped on the desktop, gazing at Ben Hastings with the expression of a man who had just bitten into a green quince.

'Wonderful,' he said to the captain. 'Just exactly what we needed—some damned cloak-and-dagger angle. Howarth say anything else?'

Hastings returned Forster's sour look with his customary, and very deceptive, expression of imperturbable serenity. 'What kind of a question is that, Reg? You know perfectly well those people don't even talk in their sleep. No, he didn't say anything else, and my experience with CIA men is that they don't even talk to themselves. As for Oberhauser, I'll make a wild guess: he was either a spy for *us* or for *them*, and it could be either way. Anyone with his kind of a background, could turn out to be anything—anything at all.' Hastings arose, tipped cigar ash in the only ashtray in the office—on John Blaine's desk—and straightened up saying, 'Don't look so upset, Reg. With any luck at all, Howarth and the CIA will lift this thing right out of our hands. We're cops, not international agents. We try to catch murderers, not assassins.'

John scowled slowly. 'What the hell's the difference?'

Hastings, on his way to the door, shot John

a look. 'There is one, John. Think about it.'

After the captain had departed Forster said, 'I knew it. I felt it in my bones, right from the start. We couldn't be lucky enough to have a clean, open-and-shut murder. Not with this guy.' He poked in his top drawer for the report on Oberhauser, and glanced up only when John pitched it across to him. As he settled himself to re-read the rather thick report, he said, 'Has ballistics called yet?' and when John replied negatively, Forster then said, 'That's not going to matter anyway. Neither are fingerprints, if any are found, and all the rest of the routine stuff. For this guy, we're going to put on dark glasses, false beards, and meet secretly on dark nights ... Damn it all, anyway.'

Blaine took the cue and ambled out of the office. He and Forster had worked together, now, for four years. In that length of time John Blaine had discovered exactly what kind of a deep and complicated nature his partner had. He had also learned that when Reg got into one of those surly moods, and turned all his considerable astuteness to an assignment, the best thing to do was not be there at all for an hour or two.

He went across the street for coffee, and stayed for lunch, then, on his way back an hour later, stopped at Communications on the off chance that an answer to his ID check might have come in from the FBI.

23

It had, and it also referred Wilshire Division's Homicide Bureau to the Central Intelligence Agency, with a red urgency. Otherwise, the FBI report noted that Irene Oberhauser was Harold Oberhauser's second wife, that she had once been a dancer in Las Vegas, had been married twice before, and gave her vitals as being forty years of age, five feet and eight inches in height, her weight being one hundred and thirty pounds, and concluded with a list of her employers prior to her marriage to Harold Oberhauser, almost all of which John Blaine told the operations office in Communications, was obviously a whitewash; that LAPD could have got the same information from the Motor Vehicles Department in the state capital, up at Sacramento. Then John went ambling back upstairs, unlighted cigar in his mouth, thinking unkind thoughts because any FBI report could have done much better than this.

Forster was standing at the window when John entered, and wordlessly tossed down the report. Forster only glanced at it as he said, 'Which one?'

'Irene Oberhauser.'

Forster turned back to his window-gazing. 'Did you have lunch?' he asked, and when Blaine replied that he had, Forster went to the desk, sat down, shoved the report on Irene Oberhauser aside, unread, and smiled at Blaine.

Immediately, John audibly sighed. He knew that look.

'We need a list of Oberhauser's closest friends,' Forster announced. 'You needn't bother with the guy next door who borrows the lawn-mower, or the industrial associate who drops round after hours now and then for a highball in the executive suite. What we want is the identity of everyone who has been close to Oberhauser for the past three or four years,' as Forster settled forward finally to pick up the Irene Oberhauser report, he also said, 'See if you can expedite the coroner's report, John, and the minute that dope comes through on Kramer, bring it up, will you?'

John arose, a trifle annoyedly. At the door he looked back. 'All of a sudden you're beginning to like this, aren't you,' he said. 'An hour ago you were sunk in gloom. Now, you're going out this afternoon and get measured for a cloak, and buy yourself a lousy dagger.' He passed out into the corridor with only Reg Forster's smile, more enigmatic than usual, in his immediate memory.

Down in the mail section there was nothing for Homicide from the coroner's office, so Blaine put in a call. All he got by way of an answer was a short-tempered, acid reminder that Los Angeles had its cold-storage vaults full, and there was just so much money allocated by the city fathers for the hiring of doctors to perform autopsies and post-mortem examinations, and if Wilshire Division thought it was some kind of special agency entitled to preferential attention, it was as wrong as all hell; when the Oberhauser thing was finished, the report would be sent along—through channels!

John put down the telephone, lit a cigar, put a soulful gaze upon a very shapely, very dark girl, and when even this satisfying view did not lift his spirits, he thought about his vacation, which would not be due for another two months, although he would have liked very much to have had it starting right now.

Then he went along to Communications to try another interception before the communiqué, if it had arrived, was sent along to Records and Identification, and after being told that there was nothing on anyone named Joseph Kramer, he went out, climbed into the car, and started out over the same ground previously covered, in the hope that someone along the line would be able to supply him with names of Oberhauser's close friends.

It had not been a very productive day, for a fact, but at least the air was clear, for a change, and the sky was a lovely shade of pale blue, and someone had pinned the sun up there where it was supposed to be, so that all the smog-clotted denizens of Los Angeles could raise their eyes and be assured that somewhere, all the natural order of things was still in perfect accord with the Grand Destiny, whatever the grand destiny was.

He did not get out to Westwood. Using the transceiver to report his bearing and destination, he was instructed to return at once to his office.

That was all; no reason given, just return. John coasted to an intersection, patiently waited until he could safely violate the traffic laws without any black-and-whites in view, then made the U-turn and started back, keeping a wary eye on the rear-view mirror just in case a black-and-white had seen his violation, because traffic cruisers delighted in citing fellow officers, but most particularly, those in civilian clothes bearing the identification of detectives. Not that John would have had to appear in traffic court. Worse, he would receive a strong reprimand, and it would go into his record that he'd broken a traffic law.

No traffic cruiser appeared, but it would not have surprised him one bit if it had; so far, it had been that kind of a day.

He drove moderately, neither imbued with any particular sense of urgency, or of curiosity. The emergency teams drove fast, Code Three with sirens screaming, homicide policemen, like undertakers and the coroner's people, rarely had occasion to hasten; their customers were not, as a general rule, in need of speedy attention.

As for curiosity, John Blaine had been a policeman even longer than he had been a

27

detective; after about the thousandth surprise, a man no longer responded to curiosity as he once had.

CHAPTER FOUR

IRENE OBERHAUSER

Ordinarily the tempo of existence on the second floor of Wilshire Division seemed to be most hectic in the morning, and the second floor's philosopher, Reg Forster, had attributed this to the fact that everyone is fresher, then; more able to pull inward to the Homicide Bureau's vortex, wavelengths of action and activity, in its forms of purest energy.

But the rules were evidently flexible. Occasionally there would also be a hectic afternoon. When John Blaine shuffled into the office and saw Forster on the telephone across the room, he also felt the vibrant emanations, which meant, of course, that today at least, the tempo had been reversed; the day had started out dull, and was now going to end up hectic. He lit a cigar and sat down at his desk to seek an annoying hangnail until Reg put aside the telephone.

It was a moderately long wait, he never found the hangnail, and when Forster finally replaced the telephone he said, 'Do you suppose we need to be exorcized ?'

Blaine sat and gravely considered his friend. 'I had it done when I was about a week old. Didn't you?'

Forster blinked. ' . . . *Exorcized*, I said . . . oh forget it, it was a bad joke anyway. We're not going to be able to get rid of the Oberhauser case after all. How does that grasp you?'

Blaine was not disturbed. 'What of it? Whoever said we were going to get rid of it? You just assumed, because some CIA clown was supposed to show up—'

'That's it, John. Mr Fred Howarth won't be showing up.'

Blaine aimed a finger. 'A *hah*! The diabolical Black Hand got him!'

'He was scuttled in Chicago when a shuttle-copter cracked up on landing and Mr Howarth sustained a broken leg and multiple bruises.'

Blaine was still not very impressed. 'Was he the only agent they had? Seems to me I read somewhere that the CIA's got 'em in the woodwork all over the world.'

Forster shrugged. 'They'll come up with another one, no doubt about it, since they showed such an interest in the Oberhauser affair, but LAPD can't wait, can it?'

Blaine was prepared to sit comfortably and discuss this aspect. 'Why can't we wait? We don't have anything to go on, so we'll *have* to wait.'

Forster glanced at his wrist. 'Mrs Oberhauser called to say she would be coming down this afternoon.'

Blaine was unimpressed. 'Is that why you called me back, to sit in on the interrogation of an over-age belly-dancer? Okay; she made a rapid recovery from being prostrated, earlier, to coming down here today.'

Reg said, 'Some people mourn a long while, some mourn a short while.' His eyes assumed the tough scepticism of a career detective. 'Some mourn during a bout with their doctor, and begin recovering rapidly from melancholia after a bout with their lawyer. Oberhauser, I should imagine, was a wealthy man. Money has a way of assuaging the hell out of grief.'

'You're shooting her down and you haven't even met her.'

'I am *not* shooting her down. I'm just naturally cynical. And that's not why I called you back.' He held a report in his hands. 'Joseph is spelt with an 'f' not a "ph". Josef Kramer, age fifty-two, three years service with the *Heimwehr*, then service with the *Wehrmacht*, captured outside Moscow, repatriated by exchanging identification tags with a dying chaplain.' Reg looked up. 'It's more detailed, you can read the rest of it yourself, but that's the gist of Kramer's background.'

John reached to accept the Kramer report, as he said, rather plaintively, '*Heimwehr*,

Wehrmacht, Obersturmbannfuhrer, sauerkraut *und* pretzels. How did these guys get into the country in the first place? I used to think Mexicans and South Americans were off-beat enough, but after a while you get so's you can understand some of their language—but *this . . .*'

Blaine shook his head, glanced at the Kramer report, then repeated the question. 'How *did* they get in?'

'Through sponsorship,' explained Forster. 'For Kramer it wouldn't have been too hard. He was a *former* enemy. I'd guess he showed the proper contrition, too, but mainly, his service record, which you've got in your hands, showed long, hard, and honourable service. All he needed was a US citizen to sponsor him, and he could come over and take out papers, which he did. Oberhauser's a different story; even with a sponsor, those SS people had two strikes against them. But someone sponsored him, and whoever that sponsor was, he had to be high enough to pull strings. I've got an enquiry out on this sponsor. As for Kramer— he's the best suspect we've got, John. He had the opportunity, he sure as hell had the training to shoot someone, and if we can figure out a motive, we can go to the City Attorney for support.' Forster smiled. 'But I don't think Kramer did it.'

John, reading the lengthy Kramer report, looked up slowly. 'This guy was a one-man army. He went all through that damned war picking up citations, wound-stripes, and came out a—a—*Hauptsharfuhrer*. Catch that accent; pretty good, eh? What the hell is a *Hauptsharfuhrer*?'

'Sergeant-major.'

Blaine scowled. 'Where did you learn all this crap?'

'Look on the back page in the footnotes,' replied Forster.

Blaine did not turn to the page, he went back to glancing down the close-spaced, lengthy report as he murmured, half to himself, that Joseph Kramer must have had a charmed life.

Irene Oberhauser arrived, escorted through the maze of offices by a police-woman. She was a tall woman, handsome, with pale blue eyes, an arresting figure, and a degree of poise that preceded her into the little office. She was expensively, but unostentatiously, dressed, and although her wristwatch was studded with diamonds, that was her only piece of jewellery. As John brought up a chair for her, she smiled at them both, apologizing for not having been able to see them when they came to her home.

She sat, crossed one leg over the other leg, showed charm to John Blaine, and showed wariness towards Reg Forster, as she said, 'I can guess why you called to see me, but as Joseph told you, it's impossible to imagine why anyone would want to kill Harold.'

Reg did not have John Blaine's charm, but

32

he turned on what charm he did have, by smiling as he said, 'I'm interested in how you met your husband, Mrs Oberhauser. Where you met him, and how much you know of his earlier life.'

She proved to be perceptive as well as beautiful; she disposed of the first two questions swiftly, to get to the third question, which she obviously viewed as the one Homicide was most interested in. She said, 'I met Harold while I was an entertainer in Las Vegas. The way we met was commonplace enough; after my act he sent me orchids and a note. I went out with him. Later, we were married ... About his earlier life—you mean as a German army officer, don't you?'

Reg kept smiling while he nodded.

'He told me all about that. You should understand that he grew up in an environment we in America have never known. He was indoctrinated while he was still quite young, and, as he told me, like all youths, he was both patriotic and impressionable. His family had been of the lesser nobility for centuries, Inspector. They had been soldiers for generations. Harold was a good German and a good soldier. You and I, well, we have trouble understanding something like that, but for Harold and millions like him, it was perfectly rational and acceptable ... He never made excuses; he believed in his country, and he obeyed orders ... Only after the war, did he

33

really begin to question Hitler's motives.'

Reg's smile was fixed in place. Listening to this beautiful woman defend her dead husband, was like reaching back through a lot of musty records and coming up with the standard alibi, or excuse, of every war-criminal. But that did not really more than passingly claim his attention. He said, 'Did he tell you who sponsored him for entry into the United States, Mrs Oberhauser?'

The pale blue eyes remained fixed on Forster's face. 'I believe it was a Doctor Brown, but you see, Inspector, we didn't discuss all that very often. My husband became an American citizen, and launched his manufacturing business, and from that day on, he rarely talked about the war, or Germany, or any of the things in his former life. He was a kindly, understanding man, highly thought of by just about everyone. He received honours from—'

'Kramer,' interjected Forster. 'Joseph Kramer, Mrs Oberhauser.'

The widow paused, checked up short by this abrupt switch in their talk. After a moment she said, 'My husband found Kramer among the work-force at the factory. His Personnel Director, Mr Paulus, brought Kramer to my husband's attention, and Harold read the personnel dossier, and brought Kramer home as his chauffeur and handyman.' The widow smiled slightly. 'I remember the first time I ever heard them speak together in German. Joseph caught his hand in the garage door and swore in German. My husband, who was in the garden, walked over and—I don't know what he said; I don't understand German—but I knew that tone of voice. When he was through, Joseph answered him in English. I was also in the garden. Joseph said, "You are right. Even the language belongs to the past." I never heard them speak in German again, and my husband, who had no accent at all because he learned to speak English as well as German as a small boy in school, never spoke German.' The little amused smile lingered. 'One time a college professor we know socially—he's a neighbour—came over to offer my husband a bottle of imported German beer. He said something in German, and my husband answered him in English. He said—"You are wrong, Henry, American beer is much better." The amused blue eyes, fixed steadily on Reg Forster, gradually lost their look of humour. 'My husband was an *American*, Inspector.' The way she said this made it obvious that she considered this aspect of the conversation ended.

Forster sighed, leaned on his desk, and allowed the talk to drift a little by asking about her husband's business affairs, but he got very little, because Irene Oberhauser did not seem to know very much. As she said, after her marriage to Harold Oberhauser, she cut all ties with her former life in Nevada, and concentrated on being a good wife, and the manageress of their home, which, she told Forster, were things which required all her time. She only listened when her husband had infrequently mentioned business matters, but her interest was not really captured very much. Her husband had been a good provider, and a popular man, those things she knew and was proud of. As for who might have killed him, she simply had no idea at all, but was inclined to believe it was either a madman, or perhaps a killer who aimed at the wrong target, perhaps, she said, it had been a case of mistaken identity.

Forster was sympathetic, and John Blaine offered to get Mrs Oberhauser a cup of coffee from the wardroom, which she declined, with a glance at John, then, gathering her gloves and handbag, she looked steadily at Reg as though expecting to be dismissed. He arose, smiling again, and saw her to the door with a murmured apology for having inconvenienced her by this trip to Wilshire Division, and after closing the door, he turned thoughtfully back to his desk, sat down, and said, 'What do you think, John?'

Blaine gave a predictable answer. 'I'll bet she was something to see as a belly-dancer. Nicest legs I've seen in a long time.'

Reg sat down, and said, 'How did she know I was the senior inspector?'

Blaine blinked. 'What do you mean?'

'From the moment she came through that door, John, she was concentrating on me. She only looked at you twice, and she never spoke directly to you.' Reg leaned, scooped up the telephone, punched a button, and asked the woman who answered down in Reception if anyone down there had mentioned that Inspector Forster was in charge, upstairs. The answer was negative. All Mrs Oberhauser had said, when she walked in, was that she had an appointment to see Inspector Forster; no one down there had mentioned Forster's status.

Reg put down the telephone as John Blaine offered an explanation. 'When we were out at her place yesterday, talking to Kramer, you did most of the talking. He could have told her that, and she'd naturally assume you were the head man.'

Reg nodded slowly. 'That's my point, John. Someone sure as hell told her, and someone sure as hell briefed her. Kramer was her husband's flunkey. As a general thing, people in her position don't have conferences with their flunkies, do they? But I think she did. The next question is—why?'

CHAPTER FIVE

A FRESH DEVELOPMENT

Ben Hastings happened to be down in Communications when Forster's enquiry about Oberhauser's sponsor, Doctor Brown, came through. He personally brought it upstairs. Reg and John were having their first cup of coffee of the morning, and when Captain Hastings handed Reg the communiqué, Forster carefully set his cup aside, read the slip of paper, then looked up at Blaine. 'I've got a glimmer. This guy who sponsored Oberhauser for entry and citizenship was a physicist, Doctor Henry Brown.'

Hastings and Blaine waited.

'This report gives two names, Doctor Henry Brown, and Doctor Heinrich Braun.'

John finished his coffee and lit a cigar. Reg turned to open the window as he said, 'John, yesterday Mrs Obehauser told us a neighbour, a college professor, I think she said he was, brought over some kraut beer and spoke to her husband in German.' Reg smiled. 'Do a little checking will you, and see if this professor is by any chance Doctor Henry Brown, formerly Doctor Heinrich Braun.'

Blaine's expression underwent a radical change, from his normal passive, sometimes stolid look, to a look of dawning interest and respect. He turned, with a short nod to Captain Hastings, and left the office. Hastings sauntered to a chair, sat down, gazed thoughtfully at Reg Forster for a moment, then dryly said, 'You're getting involved, which is a very good thing. I like that in my people.'

Forster's stare turned wary as he faced the older man. When Hastings offered even an oblique compliment, there was usually something behind it. Usually, but not always, and that was what kept Forster off balance, until Hastings spoke again.

'The CIA is sending out another man, to replace the chap who broke a leg in Chicago. He should be showing up by tomorrow night.' Hastings smiled. 'You should be glad.'

Forster answered forthrightly. 'Yesterday, but not so glad today. I'm beginning to get a "feel" about this Oberhauser thing.'

Hastings's benign smile lingered. 'Good. You'll be able to give the new man a helping hand.' He arose and got to the door before Forster spoke again.

'If he's new to the West Coast, perhaps you could arrange to have him taken on a sightseeing trip for a day or two, Captain.'

Hastings turned in the doorway. He was no longer smiling. Instead, he was studying Forster from the width of the little room, with a thoughtful expression. Finally he commented. 'I think it's their ball game, not ours. Reg, we're not spy-catchers.'

'What's the difference, Ben? They get different training than we do, and they function without regional limitations, otherwise LAPD's got jurisdiction. Oberhauser is *our* murder victim, more than theirs. Just a couple of days?'

Hastings continued to gaze at his subordinate a moment or two longer, then, without committing himself either way, but with a slight shrug, he turned away, closed the door, and went sauntering up the corridor in the direction of his own office, while Forster retrieved the Kramer report from Blaine's desk, and took it to the window to read again. Wherever the murder of Harold Oberhauser might lead, Josef Kramer looked like a fair point of origin for it to lead from.

There was another report in his mail-basket. He had already studied it, and it only showed that Oberhauser Industry's bright young man, Ray Johnson, was exactly what he had seemed to be, an ambitious college graduate with a knack for polishing the right apples among Oberhauser Industry's executives. Johnson had no police record, lived modestly but well with a wife and two small children, between Westwood and Santa Monica, and as far as could be discovered, was an exact prototype of what he professed to be.

Time would tell about Johnson, the same as it would probably tell about some of the other colourless people Harold Oberhauser had been associated with. Only Joseph Kramer stood out, and even he did not really stand out very much, at least not on paper, but there was Forster's dawning interest in the man.

John Blaine called in from the Administrative Section of the University of California at Los Angeles, UCLA, whose huge sprawling Westwood campus covered more ground than the incorporated environs of many modest cities. Henry Brown, was, in fact, Heinrich Braun. He was an eminent physicist, which was all they knew at UCLA. But, John said over the telephone, there was an interesting little quirk, which he'd dug up through the Immigration Department; Brown-Braun, according to his citizenship-application dossier in Washington, had been a relative of Adolf Hitler's mistress, Eva Braun, and, John said, speaking condescendingly, as everyone knew, Eva Braun had died in the Berlin bunker with Adolf Hitler, and, also as everyone certainly knew, her brother, also named Braun, had been shot in the head at Hitler's orders, shortly before Hitler and Eva Braun had also perished, because he had been suspected of treacherously trying to contact the Allies with a view towards playing a role in the German capitulation of 1945.

After John had explained all this, Forster said, 'Okay; now I've had my history lesson for today. But if Eva and Hitler, and this other

Braun, died about thirty years ago—what's the connection between all that, and Harold Oberhauser?'

Blaine's reply came slowly. 'I don't know. You asked me to find out if Braun and Brown were the same. They are. As for the rest of it— I guess it just shows we're taking a hand in something pretty damned historic.' John paused a moment, then rather dejectedly said, 'Yeah, I know; I might as well come on in and get to work on something else.'

Forster chuckled as he replaced the telephone, and resumed his study of the Kramer report. Almost leisurely, he put in a call to the office of the City Attorney, and was told that, in response to his query, yes, the City Attorney was *very* interested in the Oberhauser matter, and, yes, enquiries had been coming down from the mayor's office, and even from the Governor's mansion, up in Sacramento, about four hundred miles distant, as well as from the offices of a great number of business people, politicians, and of course, the labour people, all wanting to know what steps were being taken speedily to bring the killer of Harold Oberhauser to the bar.

Forster did not say what steps were being taken; he had called to *get* information, not *give* it. What he specifically wanted to know was whether anyone in particular might have called, perhaps a union leader, another industrialist, someone whose interest might have been exceptionally keen.

None had. At least as far as the assistant City Attorney Forster spoke to, knew, there had been no display of particular interest, unless it had come from the City Attorney himself, who had made it clear to his staff that he wanted this Oberhauser case very much. He was not very far from having to begin the struggle for re-election; if he could bring off a conviction in such a sensational case as the one involving Harold Oberhauser, the well-known and well-liked industrialist, it would be a very gratifying thing.

Forster agreed. It would indeed be a very gratifying thing. Then he rang off, finished the Kramer report, arose to adjust his tie and leave the office on his way across the street for something to eat.

John Blaine found him over there when he returned from Westwood, and sighed himself into the same small booth, not for food, but for coffee and conversation, which was not as fattening, and John had to mind his weight.

He produced a small wallet-size photograph of a rather lanky looking man with pale eyes, light hair, a long face, and steel-rimmed glasses. 'Henry Brown,' he said, and fished in a jacket pocket. 'I've got a tape of his voice, too.'

Forster was surprised. 'How did you get that?'

Blaine tossed the small plastic container atop the table. 'Easy,' he replied. 'The

43

instructors out there tape their lectures. Students who missed out, or who want to re-hear the thing, can buy these for a buck. So, I paid my buck and brought Henry along with me. We can play it in the lab, if you'd like.'

Forster's meal came, along with Blaine's coffee. John had to re-pocket the tape because the table was so small that Reg's dishes nearly covered it. After the waitress was gone, and after he had tasted his coffee, Blaine said, 'Anything new?'

Forster chewed with vigour before answering. 'Just one thing; we want a tail on Kramer.'

'For a guy who said he didn't believe Kramer hit Oberhauser, you're sure interested in him,' stated John, wistfully eyeing the large shrimp salad in front of Forster.

Reg's retort was predictable. 'Like I told you, we don't have anyone else. And I don't think he killed Oberhauser. But right now our biggest obstacle is trying to get past this ten-foot-high wall of solid admiration, and into the lethal weedpatch which has to exist beyond it, somewhere.' Forster paused to look steadily at Blaine. 'John, it's that, or go back to Neuengamme and work forward until we reach 1975, wading through corpses and vengeful relatives up to our ears; people who by now are scattered all over the world.'

John finished his coffee and picked up the small photograph of Henry Brown. 'Okay, put that way, I'll opt for Joseph Kramer too. Incidentally, I'll run Henry Brown through the grinder when we go across the street, but from the looks of this guy I can't imagine any army giving him a rifle and letting him march behind other soldiers. Did you notice how thick those glasses are? Like the bottoms from a pair of Coke bottles.'

John pocketed the picture, watched Forster eat for a while, then said, 'Disgusting,' and started to leave the table.

Reg glanced up, 'Are you dieting again?'

'Do I usually drink one lousy cup of coffee in here?'

Reg slowly shook his head; Blaine got irritable when he was on one of his periodic diets. 'What do you think of a tail on Mrs Oberhauser?'

John hung there, beside the table, while he turned this over in his mind, then he said, 'It can't do any harm. Want me to set it up with Cap; you'll be another half hour eating all that stuff. I'm going over to the office and start to work on Henry Brown; I can see Cap too.'

Forster smiled. 'Good idea. And John . . . ?'

'Yeah.'

'You could eat a shrimp salad, it's not fattening.'

'Isn't it? You better get a calorie-counter. That mayonnaise'll plug up your arteries with cholesterol every time.'

After Blaine had walked through the noisy

restaurant towards the roadway, Forster examined his delicious seafood meal with fresh interest, then went ahead and ate it all anyway.

Later, on his way back across the busy roadway, he met Captain Hastings. They walked a short distance together with the captain saying, 'The Commissioner called me this morning. I think someone reached him from either the mayor's office or FBI headquarters in Washington. He was nervous about the Oberhauser affair.'

Forster said candidly that he was also nervous about the Oberhauser affair, then he asked for surveillance for Irene Oberhauser and Joseph Kramer, and, perhaps because it sounded good, Captain Hastings assented. Then he left, heading for the restaurant, and Forster got back to the upstairs office just as John was returning from the large office at the west end of the hall. John reported no success with Captain Hastings, because he was not in his office.

Forster said, 'Forget it. I met him outside. He agreed to the surveillance.' Then Forster opened the window behind his desk in anticipation of a lighted cigar, and sure enough, as John related that he had put Brown-Braun through the identification and information procedure, he lit up.

John also said, 'The ballistics report's on your desk. The coroner's report is there too. Can you guess?'

46

Forster glanced at the desk as he answered. 'Yeah; bullet fired from a silenced weapon, medium calibre, range deduced from velocity: close. Wound instantaneously fatal.'

'That's all?'

Forster looked steadily across the room, then stepped to his desk and picked up the papers. He glanced through the ballistics report first; it was crisp, highly technical, and completely impersonal, as all such reports were. Then he read the second report, from the coroner's office, and suddenly stopped mid-way through, sat down to re-read a paragraph, and frowned as he said, 'What in the hell does this mean—uncertain identity? They don't make identifications down there, except from what we give them. That's not their—'

'That's exactly what they used, the homicide report. And they are correct.' Blaine arose, stepped to Forster's desk with two fingerprint cards. 'This is the card they made at the coroner's office, and this is our card, from the FBI. Different fingerprints, Reg.' Blaine straightened up, puffed a moment on his cigar, then returned to his desk and sat down. 'Two different sets of prints—two separate men.'

CHAPTER SIX

THE CLANGER

Forster called the assistant county coroner, which was a very good contact, except that this individual was more administrator of the sprawling office, than actual practising dissectionist, so he said he'd go downstairs and make a personal investigation, then call Forster back.

His word was good, he returned the call within fifteen minutes, and verified that the fingerprints made at the coroner's office, for their records down there, did not match with the prints furnished by Homicide, Wilshire Division and that it did not require the skill of a trained technician to see the difference.

Forster rang off, silently gazed at the two cards for a while, then raised his eyebrows at John, but Blaine had assumed his cigar-smoking, bland look, and, having said all he knew, made no move to improve that, or to spoil it, either.

Forster finally arose from his desk. 'Where is this physicist; I mean, will he be at the University today, or at home?'

'Home,' announced Blaine succinctly, also arising. 'They've got a pretty good set-up out there; I wish we had their benefits.'

'Do you know the address?'

'Yeah.'

'Then let's go talk to Doctor Brown—or whatever the hell his name is.'

As they headed out of the building, John jettisoned his cigar. He and Forster had a pact, no cigars while together in the closeness of the car. It was more than half smoked anyway.

They drove two miles before Forster said, 'Do you realize what this probably means, John?'

Blaine's answer was philosophically calm. 'Sure; somebody *was* Oberhauser, and somebody *wasn't.* The card from our files came from the FBI, which is a pretty hard source to find fault with. So—*that* card was more than likely the proper one; Oberhauser's genuine prints were on it. This other card—'

'Made from the corpse.'

'Okay—made from the corpse, shows the fingerprints of someone else, a second party.'

'So,' stated Forster, taking it up from there, 'this "someone else", this damned second party, wasn't Harold Oberhauser.'

Blaine held up a hand. 'Wait. One of them wasn't Harold Oberhauser, but at this point, we don't know which one wasn't. Maybe the guy at the morgue was Oberhauser. Maybe the guy who made the original prints for the FBI was the fake Harold Oberhauser.'

Forster adjusted his sun-glasses against the fierce, smog-laden sunshine, and waggled his head a little. Until they pulled up out front of a very attractive, very neat and handsomely landscaped cottage only a few doors from the Oberhauser place, Forster kept silent. But as they were alighting he said, 'If the dead guy downtown isn't the real Harold Oberhauser, John, then he'd either been playing the role for several years, or else the woman he was married to, plus Kramer, and the Lord knows who else, knew there was an impersonation.'

Blaine continued bland. 'Not necessarily. He and the woman were only married four or five years, and Kramer had only been his camp-robber for a couple or three years. If he was an impersonator, he'd only have had to be one for about five years. That's not such a long time.'

They were met on the emerald lawn out front of the residence by the lanky, pale-eyed, rumpled man of the snapshot, and when he saw the ID folders, he introduced himself as Henry Brown, Doctor Henry Brown, actually, but he deprecatingly smiled away the title as he shook hands then escorted his callers to the shade of a flower-garnished very delightful flag-stoned patio. There, inviting the detectives to be seated, he smiled and said, 'I wondered . . . I thought you would canvass the neighbourhood, sooner or later.'

Doctor Brown had no accent at all. Forster, for the most part unsmiling and still troubled by the recently-revealed mystery of *two* Harold

Oberhausers, asked several innocuous, unimportant questions, to set his host at ease, then he said, 'You are a naturalized citizen, Doctor?' and for the first time, Brown's smile got a little strained.

Peering from behind thick lenses, he said, 'I give you credit for doing your homework, Inspector. Yes, I am a naturalized citizen. Would you care to see my papers?'

Forster didn't care about the papers. 'You were born in Germany?'

Brown's smile faded completely, now. 'Yes. And the rest of it you probably also know. I served in the special weapons section, research ... I helped perfect the flying bomb and several other innovations. I was at Peenemunde when the war ended ... Peenemunde, you will recall, was where Germany was carrying out nuclear research. One more year, gentlemen, and Germany would have anticipated the United States with the first nuclear bomb ... It would have been a different war, then, eh?'

John Blaine offered a dry comment about that. 'Maybe, Doctor. Where would you have dropped it—London or Paris?'

Brown coloured slightly, considered John for a moment of prickly silence, then smiled again, and spoke forth with a jovial ring to his rather pleasant, accentless voice. 'Well; but of course that was over so long ago, eh? And for the best, as things have turned out. Well

. . . about Harold Oberhauser; what can I tell you?'

Forster asked how long Brown had known the dead man, and got a slight scowl of concentration before getting an answer. 'Since I bought this house, I'd say about three or four years. But we were not on the first-name basis until a little over a year ago when Harold admired my ranunculus.' Brown smiled at the two blank looks he got. 'There; those flowers in the bed over there. Harold was really a rose fancier. He had a magnificent display of them out back, you know. It was the vigour and the size of my ranunculus that impressed him. We became fairly friendly after that.'

'You did not know him in Germany, then?'

The pale eyes widened. 'Oh no; you see, we had nothing in common over there. Well; of course the common cause, but you shared that with everyone. No, I did not know Harold Oberhauser until I moved here, and really became acquainted with him a year or so ago.'

'But you knew he was German,' murmured Forster, and Doctor Brown's reply was accompanied with a slight deprecating gesture.

'The name, Inspector, and—well—there were other things, the bearing, the features. And there was his man, Kramer. I spoke to him several times in German. He told me a little; that Mr Oberhauser was a naturalized citizen, the same as I was, and of course the same as Kramer was.'

Forster said, 'What else did Kramer tell you?'

'Nothing much. If you mean anything personal about the Oberhausers, not a word, really.' Doctor Brown arose. 'Lemonade, gentlemen? I'd offer beer but you wouldn't accept that on duty, would you?'

They also declined the lemonade, so Brown sank down again, sitting upon the edge of his lawn chair, long, thin hands clasped in front of him. He seemed entirely at ease, interested, even a little curious, but quite poised.

Reg said, 'Did you know Mrs Oberhauser, by any chance?'

Brown made that little deprecatory gesture again, half apologetic, half uncertain. It seemed to be a habit of his. 'Only to speak to. I went over there a few times for a patio supper with them. Yes, you could say I knew her, but not really very well. We would nod, sometimes, when we met out front in our gardens, but—I think I could say, there was more aloofness to her than to her husband. Perhaps because she was a married woman, I can't really say.' Brown smiled. 'I am a single man. I can't claim to be much of an authority on women.'

'Did Mr Oberhauser speak German with you, Doctor Brown?' Forster asked casually, as he got ready to arise.

'As a matter of fact, Inspector, he didn't. One time he told me very clearly that he did not use that language at all.' Brown made his

53

little deprecatory gesture and also arose. 'It was quite acceptable to me; you must understand that a great many of us who were in the war, and emigrated, have blocked out that part of our lives completely.'

As they strolled back round front Forster had one more question. 'In the four or five years that you knew Harold Oberhauser, did he always seem the same to you?'

Brown stopped in his tracks. 'The same? I don't understand, Inspector.' Suddenly Brown's puzzled look vanished. 'Oh; you mean, upset or worried, something like that. Well; he was an executive of a very large and successful business, wasn't he? I suppose, from time to time, he seemed a little different.' Brown resumed pacing along towards the parked departmental car as he spoke. 'I can't recall, off hand, any particular incident, but I'm sure he must have seemed ... You are wondering, perhaps, if he had seemed different for the week or so prior to the murder—maybe because he was apprehensive? No, nothing like that. He was his usual good-natured, amiable self.'

When they had shaken hands again, then departed, John said, 'I'll say one thing for that guy, he sure jumps to conclusions, then sounds off about them until you can't get a word in edgewise.'

Forster hadn't heard. He said, 'We're going to need another surveillance.'

Blaine looked round sharply. 'On him?'

'Yeah.'

'He didn't say anything, Reg. That guy was letter-perfect, even about the interlude we already knew about, when Oberhauser chewed him out for talking German.'

Forster loosened his tie, settled comfortably in the seat beside Blaine, and blew out a big, tired breath, before saying, 'John, those were calendulas, not ranunculus.'

Blaine stopped at a red light, put a long, quizzical look at the slouched man beside him, then, when the light turned green for them to drive on, he muttered a mild curse.

When they got back to Wilshire Division, Captain Hastings had left a note on Forster's desk. He wanted to see them both. Forster snugged up his tie, straightened his jacket, and led the way.

Hastings had the prettiest receptionist in Homicide, which didn't really have to be all much of a compliment, because she was almost the only receptionist in Homicide, but nevertheless, she was very handsome, quite dark, and her name was Virginia. She smiled at them, nodded towards the closed door, and when they passed through, Ben Hastings was just replacing the telephone. He gestured towards chairs.

'There's a damned screw-up,' he blurted out. 'That's not the same Harold Oberhauser at the morgue that the FBI has records on.'

Forster acknowledged this mildly. 'We know, Captain. We turned up the fingerprint cards this morning.'

'Well; what are you doing about it?'

Forster loosened in his chair. 'I'd say we're still getting over the shock.'

Hastings leaned on his desk. 'Well, I'll give you another shock, then. I got a team of medical wizards from County General Hospital to go down there and put that corpse through its paces. The call I was just finishing when you walked in, was from their head man. The corpse is six or seven years younger than Harold Oberhauser was, according to his Immigration and FBI records, and as melodramatic as this may sound, the corpse had had plastic surgery.'

John leaned forward. 'On his face?'

'Yes.'

John continued to lean, staring at Ben Hastings. 'Okay. Then *this* one is *not* Harold Oberhauser. Right?'

Hastings would not commit himself. 'That's a reasonable guess, John. Most of it I suppose could be faked, but not the five or six years.'

Reg arose and stepped to a closed window where slanted venetian blinds filtered out the sun's rays but not the sun's light. He turned, over there, and said, 'Digressing for a moment, Ben: we want a surveillance put on Doctor Henry Brown.'

Hastings did not even look up. 'All right.

56

You've got his address and particulars?'

Blaine fished forth a small notebook and wrote in it, then ripped out the piece of paper and put it upon the desk.

Captain Hastings only glanced at the note. He threw himself back in the swivel chair and looked at the acoustic ceiling as he said, to no one in particular, 'Where the hell is that CIA spook? *This* one I'd like very much to get rid of. And fast.'

CHAPTER SEVEN

FORSTER'S DAWNING SUSPICION

There was one more thing Reg Forster wanted to do, but he was leary of asking Hastings about it; he wanted bugs put on the telephones at the Brown and Oberhauser residences, but right then, bugging and tapping telephones was not viewed by anyone, even the police, with great favour, thanks to President Nixon and his Watergate imbroglio. In the end, Reg did not make the request, but on the way back down the corridor beside John Blaine, he said, 'We're not going to get anywhere on this, John, until we can come up with a way through the sauerkraut curtain.'

Blaine, bland again, said, 'At least we've eliminated that Neuengamme concentration camp angle. What we've got now is a mystery, but it's all right here, in Los Angeles, not in Poland or France or the Soviet Union.'

Forster held their office door for Blaine to precede him, and said, 'What the hell are you talking about? We haven't eliminated anyone, we've simply come up with more of a lousy mystery. I'll tell you what it's beginning to look like to me; some kind of cloak-and-dagger stuff. Like Oberhauser wasn't just a repentant Nazi, and a wealthy industrialist basking under a freshly turned over new leaf. In fact, I don't think that's Oberhauser on the coroner's slab at all.'

Blaine picked up the fingerprint card from Reg's desk and turned back towards the door with it. 'I'll run this through and find out just who the hell that guy really is.'

'Really was,' growled Forster, sinking down in his chair and picking up the other card. As John departed, the telephone rang and a crisp masculine voice said, 'Inspector Forster? This is Dumas, down the hall. My partner and I have drawn the surveillance of Joseph Kramer, from Captain Hastings, who instructed me to call you for particulars or idiosyncrasies.'

'Just one,' growled Reg. 'If there's trouble, don't close with that guy; he could crush an iron elephant if he could get his arms around it.'

'That's all, Inspector?'

Forster looked at the telephone. 'What do

you mean—is that all? If I knew more I wouldn't need him under surveillance!'

Reg put down the telephone, and it immediately rang again. He picked it up and growled his name. This time the caller was John Blaine.

'This thing is getting very interesting,' he told Forster. 'As soon as someone started crying foul about those fingerprints, ID ran this card I've got through, and just received the teletype from Washington. There are no matching prints on file with the FBI. They are going to run it through the CIA, and if that doesn't turn up anything, they're going to run it through Interpol.'

Forster put down the telephone, for the second time within moments, beginning to have that same sinking sensation Captain Hastings had had earlier. He even considered calling the Los Angeles division of the CIA and demanding to know just what in the hell was delaying their man.

He did not do it, and in any case he never would have done it. He'd have *thought* about it, but he would never have gone looking for help.

A call came through from the City Attorney's office. Everyone, it seemed, had somehow learned that the man in the coroner's cold-room was probably not Harold Oberhauser, and the reaction at higher elevations was unanimously the same: stunned

59

shock, bleating enquiries, then roars of indignation accompanied with demands for immediate action of *some* kind. By quitting time Forster was thoroughly willing to chuck everything. He did not even wait until John returned from downstairs.

On the drive home to his flat it occurred to him to inaugurate a completely detailed search into the background of Harold Oberhauser, through the American Intelligence people connected with the army in Germany. It also occurred to him that if, as he was beginning to suspect, Oberhauser had been more than a naturalized citizen, an industrialist with a handsome wife, fine home, and all the creature comforts that went with such an ideal 'cover' for espionage, it did not make much sense for him to be either impersonated—or killed. Creating that kind of a cover took years and was very costly; it would not have been done with a man someone lacked faith in. Then why kill him, or, for that matter, why have him impersonated *and then killed*?

He swung up into the driveway of his apartment building, switched off the engine, and sat a long while in the sweltering heat staring straight ahead. There was a reason. There had to be a reason, since both the impersonation and the killing had taken place.

Finally, he left the car, went to his flat, undressed and took a cool shower, then went out to the small kitchen for a glass of chilled beer from the refrigerator, and with this bachelor's companion, returned to the air-conditioned living room to sit in his shorts, staring out of a tinted window in the direction of the obscured, distant hills.

The reason was not clear, because he had nothing to base it upon, but it *was* discernible, so he finished the beer, went to his bedroom to get dressed, and left the apartment to cruise back to Wilshire Division.

The night duty force was on hand, in its customary minimal peace-keeping capacity. He got up to his office without encountering anyone, once he left the lower floor. At the desk, he called Communications to inform them that calls coming in from any of the three surveillance teams need not be electronically recorded, as was customary, but could be put through to his telephone. Then he composed a letter of enquiry respecting a detailed, a *minutely* detailed, background search and report on Harold Oberhauser, and because he needed Captain Hastings's approval before going outside police channels with such an enquiry, he called the Hastings residence, and was informed that Captain Hastings was out with his bowling team, in a tournament, and would have to call Forster back when he got in.

This, Forster told himself, resignedly, was exactly in accordance with all the luck he'd had this day. He put down the telephone and went next door to the wardroom for coffee. The telephone jangled as he was passing back through the doorway from next door. He hastened to answer it. The caller was Dumas, the junior-grade detective who had drawn the assignment of keeping Joseph Kramer under surveillance.

Kramer had departed from the Oberhauser residence in one of the Oberhausers' cars, had driven nine miles to a small city park, and was now sitting on a bench reading a newspaper, evidently waiting for someone. Forster told Dumas to keep in touch, and settled the telephone with one hand while lifting the coffee cup with the other hand. He was fairly certain his other two surveillance teams would be inactive, so, when the next call came in, informing Forster that Doctor Brown had also driven away shortly before, Forster's interest heightened. He asked the general direction Brown had taken, which was also south-westerly, and as an idea began to form in his mind, he kept the second surveillance car on the line, reporting its location until Doctor Brown parked about a half mile from the same little park, alighted, and went briskly walking through the late-day dusk.

From this point on the reporting became a little less than perfect. One member of the surveillance team tailed Brown, and relayed his information back to the second member of the team in the police car, by hand transceiver. This information had then to be relayed through the radio in the car, to Reg Forster.

Forster had already guessed Brown's destination, and he was correct. The tailing officer saw Brown meet Kramer. The two men walked through the little park slowly, speaking back and forth, heads down, quite obviously seriously conversing. The tailing officer could not get close enough to eavesdrop, so he remained a lurking shadow among the trees and shrubs, keeping the two men in sight.

Forster was satisfied an eavesdrop wouldn't have helped much. If his idea was correct, Brown and Kramer would not be speaking in English anyway. Forster understood no German, and was satisfied neither of the leg-men understood German either.

He asked if Kramer had abandoned the newspaper he had been reading while sitting on the bench, and when this was confirmed, he asked that it be brought in, then he rang off, finished his coffee, tried the Hastings residence again, with no real hope, and was not disappointed when he was told that the captain had not as yet returned.

His next call was from John Blaine, who did not even verify that Forster was on the other end when he said, 'What in the hell are you doing down there tonight, that can't be done much better tomorrow?'

Forster could not truly answer that affirmatively, so he said, 'How did you know I was down here?'

'Buzzed the flat and got no answer.'

'I could have been out on a date, you know.'

Blaine's retort was dry. 'No, I don't know. Because you've had that weird expression on your face you get on it every time we come up against a hard one . . . Turned up anything?'

'Not much. Brown and Kramer had a rendezvous in a little park down near Santa Monica. They're still down there. Brown's probably telling Kramer about us visiting him today . . . And I've got a theory about Oberhauser's killing.'

There was a groaning sound of someone yawning at Blaine's end of the line, then: 'Yeah? Well, don't tell me; I like being surprised. Good night.'

Forster grinned, ran a hand across his scratchy face, started after a second cup of coffee, and was pulled back by the telephone. The rendezvous at the little park had broken up. Doctor Brown had driven away, in the direction of Santa Monica, and Kramer's surveillance team was tailing him back in the direction of the Oberhauser residence.

Forster's interest in Kramer diminished as his interest in Henry Brown increased. He told that south-bound pair of detectives not to lose Brown, and to call in as soon as Brown had settled somewhere. Then, finally, he went after the cup of coffee.

A cigarette would have gone very well with the coffee, but Forster had given up smoking

64

four years ago. Like most former smokers, though, when there was any kind of anxiety or stress, he wished for a smoke. Instead, he took the coffee back to the office and stood by the window looking out across an unattractive sea of city lights.

It was almost an hour later that two simultaneous calls came through. The one from Captain Hastings he put on 'hold', and the one from Doctor Brown's surveillance team he took sitting at the desk again.

Brown had left his car in front of a small but obviously expensive restaurant, and was now inside at a shadowy far table, ordering a meal from a large folded menu. Forster told the team to bring back the address and particulars of the restaurant, and head on in. Then he took the Hastings call, made his request for permission to send out the enquiry on Oberhauser, and got a long, long moment of thoughtful silence, before Hastings said, 'What do you need that isn't already in the report we have?'

'Details,' explained Forster. 'What we've got is a general background on the man. What I want is a *detailed*, complete, report, going back to his days in the German army.'

Hastings did not sound very enthusiastic when he said, 'All right; leave a copy on my desk. Do you know what time it is?'

Forster did not raise his wrist as he made a guess. 'Yeah, roughly ... I think Oberhauser *had* to die.'

'What did you say?'

'I said—Oberhauser *had* to die.'

Hastings's calm voice got a slight rough edge to it. 'Are you sitting in there, drinking coffee, and going into one of those damned philosophy funks of yours?'

'What I mean, Ben, is that Harold Oberhauser was involved in something, maybe without even knowing it himself, that could only be resolved by his death.'

Hastings made that same groaning, yawning sound John Blaine had made, before he said, 'Just hang up, and go home and go to bed, and first thing in the morning we'll take this whole thing up in a conference. Good night!'

Forster put down the telephone, stood up, and, because yawning is a highly contagious thing, he yawned, then he did as he had been told to do, he left the office, left the building, and finally went home, this time to stay home until morning.

CHAPTER EIGHT

DEVELOPMENTS

They did not have their conference in the morning, as Captain Hastings had advocated. Hastings was called away for a top-echelon meeting of city executives, which was entirely acceptable to Forster, who was deep into a resumé of all the background reports he'd accumulated on the involvees in the Oberhauser affair, and did not especially need the conference.

When John arrived, Forster was already two-thirds of the way through that growing stack of personal papers. John pretended to be astonished at Forster's presence and said, 'You spent the night here?'

Forster smiled, brought his associate up to date about the results of the surveillances, and explained about his Intelligence enquiry as well, then, because he'd revised his thinking about publicizing his theory on the death of Harold Oberhauser. He invited John next door for coffee, and while they were in the wardroom, John took a call from downstairs; his request for information on the fingerprints of the corpse at the morgue had come through. He excused himself and rushed down there, leaving Forster to finish the coffee alone, and afterwards to amble back to his desk, his private theory still private.

He knew enough about Kramer. At least he had pretty well memorized everything that was contained in Kramer's background and police report. A lot of details were omitted, but Kramer was coming through in all his various dimensions; whatever Forster might need later, he could probably procure. At present he was certain he knew enough about the man to fit him into the Oberhauser case where he belonged.

Doctor Brown was a temporary mystery, but Forster's view of Brown was that, despite an involvement Brown had avoided mentioning, his connection with the Oberhauser murder was not, most probably, that of a killer.

In fact, according to Forster's hunch, the killer and the reason for the killing, were not likely to be found within the confines of the Oberhauser image at all. This probably should have worried Forster a lot more than it did, since he was fearful of being dragged all over Creation if the Oberhauser affair got out of hand and went back to the days of World War Two. The reason this did not make him as anxious as it might have a couple of days before, was based upon his hunch that the key to the murder and wherever its ramifications led, was tied in with the corpse at the coroner's office; if he could make some kind of sequential sense out of *that*, he would be able to trace a murderer, without being pulled back down the years into that chaotic vortex called World War Two.

Like all theories, though, the one Forster had evolved had to be proved or disproved, and the surest method for doing either the one or the other, was to test it.

He was sitting at his desk speculating on ways of ascertaining whether he was on the right track, or not, when John returned. Without noticeable chagrin, but showing strong curiosity, Blaine announced that the corpse at the morgue had to be classified a John Doe.

'No one has a damned thing on him from his prints, which doesn't have to mean anything more than that he's an alien, probably someone who has never been in the country before. It's sure as hell not unheard of—but it's sure as hell a conspiracy, otherwise he wouldn't have been carrying Oberhauser's wallet, complete with Oberhauser's driving licence—which had one of the real Harold Oberhauser's prints on it, as is customary. So—Oberhauser, wherever he is, and whether he's alive or dead, he knew about this guy who was impersonating him.'

Forster smiled. 'You took a smart pill with your toast and coffee this morning,' he said. 'Now tell me this—*why* did Oberhauser have to die, which he obviously had to do, otherwise he would simply have dropped from sight, and this impersonator would never have had to go to all the elaborate trouble of taking his place. So, *why*; what's at the bottom of all this?'

John perched upon the edge of his desk looking a trifle annoyed. 'You write out all the variables and give them to me, and I'll feed them into a computer, and we'll see what it can come up with. Me, I'm not as interested in the whys and wherefores as I am interested in some son of a bitch who is running around Los Angeles programmed to kill people.'

Forster swung round in his chair as he said, 'I don't see him doing it again. Oberhauser was supposed to die in a manner that everyone would know about; his death was supposed to be publicized. That's all the killer was supposed to accomplish.'

'And he accomplished it,' stated Blaine, dryly.

Forster said, 'Yeah; not really, but at least as far as the newspapers are concerned, he accomplished it. Someone in the city had a murder performed for their benefit. I asked around to see if someone in particular had taken a special interest. If we could find the bird for whom Oberhauser was supposedly killed, we would probably be halfway to home-base. He'd provide a motive, and most likely, a means for us to find a murderer.'

'What did you turn up?'

'Nothing,' replied Forster. 'Short of running the whole damned population of Los Angeles County through this office for interrogation, we're not going to turn him up, either. So . . .'

'So?'

'For the time being we ignore this guy and concentrate on what we have. Did you forward those prints to Interpol?'

'Yeah. But that's not going to produce anything, and meanwhile—'

The telephone rang. Forster reached for it,

70

spoke his name, then sat hunched upon the desk, listening, as a pleasant, calm masculine voice said, 'This is Harper in Communications. Some nut just called; he said that picture of Harold Oberhauser on the front page of the newspaper day before yesterday, fit the face of some guy this nut thinks he saw yesterday up near Ventura having car trouble at a lay-by. When I told this nut to hold, that I'd put him through to the detectives who were handling the Oberhauser case, he said nothing doing, he was not going to be involved, and pulled the plug.'

Forster asked about the voice, and Harper said it was male-sounding, not too old, perhaps belonging to a man in his thirties, and seemed slightly breathless, as though the caller were very nervous over contacting the police. Harper then said, 'My guess is that he's got a record. There are lots of reasons for people not to want to identify themselves to us, but that's the best one, in my experience.'

'What did he say about the car; make, model, year, licence number?'

'Nothing, Inspector. I just gave it to you exactly as he said it. Then he rang off before I could ask any questions.'

'It's taped?'

'Yes sir. Do you want the tape sent up?'

Forster's answer was short. 'No. If we need it later we'll come for it. Thanks, Harper.' He put down the telephone, gazed a thoughtful

71

moment at John, then explained what the conversation had been about, and John Blaine's broad, low forehead turned up two deep creases. 'There are,' he said, speaking slowly, 'three of those public rest stops from the Ventura County line, before you get into the town of Ventura.' He paused, returned Forster's speculative stare for a moment, then said, 'You're projecting telepathic waves. You want me to go up there, right?'

Reg laughed. 'I thought you'd never get the thought. Yeah. Take your kit along. If he had car trouble and couldn't fix it himself—'

'I know; canvass the garages along the way.' Blaine arose. 'Well; at least it's still early morning. I ought to be able to make it back by quitting time.'

The telephone summoned Forster again, and this time the voice was not that of a man. He recognized it at once as belonging to Irene Oberhauser. She asked if she might see Inspector Forster today. He had a ready answer; he was, he said, going to be in her neighbourhood, and would stop by, which was not exactly the truth, but his conscience remained untroubled as he saw John Blaine close the door after himself, on his way out of the building, and arose to depart also.

On the drive out towards Westwood he pondered the multiple reasons why Harold Oberhauser might be driving up the coastline out of Los Angeles County into the next,

72

which was Ventura County. It was, he told himself, a pretty damned prosaic way to disappear. And where had Oberhauser got the car? Possibly from his factory, of course.

By the time he parked out front of the Oberhauser residence he had the feling that in his gropings, he was just about to reach something, was just about to lay his hands upon the key that would open the Oberhauser case. As he strolled to the wide, shady front porch, he thought wryly that it was about time for something to turn up; he could not continue to grope much longer, or there were going to be reverberations from the higher-ups.

That same grey-eyed Irish maid, with her warmly pleasant smile, opened the door. Today, though, she stepped aside for him to enter—and her smile was somehow not quite the same; it was there, but it did not have the same spontaneity. Something, anyway, was lacking from it as she took Forster on through a lovely sunken living room and out through some tall glass doors to a wonderfully fragrant and coolly soft-shadowed rear patio where Irene Oberhauser was standing, half twisted from the waist, near a squatty, dark tree with very shiny dark green leaves. As soon as the maid departed Mrs Oberhauser offered him a chair, and smilingly said, 'Where is Inspector Blaine, I thought you gentlemen always went together.'

Forster did not accept the chair as he said, 'Not always,' and tried to match her disarming smile with one equally as disarming. 'This is a beautiful patio. In fact, this is a beautiful home, Mrs Oberhauser.'

She allowed herself to be diverted by the compliment. 'Thank you, Inspector. It's taken several years to make it like this.'

'And a lot of money . . .'

Her eyes seemed to shadow momentarily, then the look passed. She went to a chair and sat down, which was his cue, so he also sat. She kept looking at him, but not with the fixed and alert wariness she'd shown at the office. This time he got the impression she wanted to say something, and was for some reason inhibited. Remembering his earlier idea of testing his theory about the entire Oberhauser matter, he said, 'I keep getting the feeling, Mrs Oberhauser, that you could help the investigation, that knowingly or not, you have information we could certainly use.'

Her reaction was slight. The only change Forster noticed, was the slight tightening of her mouth, but that was enough. He smiled. 'Not that you would knowingly conceal anything; that's not what I meant. But a wife is bound to know a lot about her husband, and somewhere, there's knowledge that would give the investigation a big boost.'

Her stone-steady eyes did not waver. 'You need a boost, Inspector?' she asked. 'I've always heard the Los Angeles police were some of the most knowledgeable and sophisticated in the country.'

He laughed. 'Knowledgeable, maybe, but I've never known a sophisticated cop.'

She smiled, and coloured slightly, which heightened her beauty in Forster's eyes. 'I didn't mean sophisticated in the social sense, Inspector. I meant it in the professional sense.'

He understood this. 'Anyway, getting back— sophisticated or not, we're bogged down. I tell you that frankly, because I need your help.'

Her steady gaze turned a little softer. It could have been understanding, sympathy, or it could have been tough irony, he was not that good an evaluator of female expressions or moods. Then she said, 'As a matter of fact, that's why I wanted to see you today, Inspector. There *is* something.' Her gaze dropped to the hands in her lap for a moment before she spoke again.

'There was a letter ... It arrived yesterday afternoon in the post ...' She leaned as though to arise. 'It's in the study, I'll get it.'

He stopped her. 'What did it say?'

'That some people in New York who have been working in conjunction with some people in Berlin, have identified my husband as *Sturmbannfuhrer* Oberhauser from the Neuengamme concentration camp, and had a file on his actions while serving at Neuengamme.'

75

She arose. 'I'll get the letter, you can read it for yourself.'

As she swept out of the patio, Forster arose and stepped over to that handsome tree with the very dark green, shiny leaves, and leaned to examine the tree, as a small voice in the back of his mind told him he was being deliberately set up. He listened to the small voice, because he always listened to it. It never offered proof, it just offered suspicions, and he always paid attention to them.

CHAPTER NINE

THE FORMING PATTERN

The letter was post-marked New York City, but there was no return-address to trace it by, and the signature was simply 'Herbert Kaplan' with no title, no address, not even any indication that 'Herbert Kaplan' whoever he might be, was affiliated with any actual group. This supposition had to be arrived at by the word 'we' in the text of the letter.

Over the years Forster had seen hundreds of crank letters, and this looked like a typical one, except that the implied threat behind the obviously antagonistic words of the letter, had already been carried out; *Sturmbannfuhrer* Oberhauser was dead. Crank letters, if they arrived subsequent to the violent death of their principal subject, became a lot more than just typical crank letters.

Forster asked if he could keep the letter, and the beautiful former belly-dancer agreed with a wave of one hand, accompanied by a look of distinct displeasure. 'I don't ever want to see it again, Inspector.'

Forster carefully pocketed the thing, then said, 'Mrs Oberhauser, almost any man who at one time was in your husband's wartime situation, would have at some time later on, down the years, said *something*; would have mentioned the possibility of revenge motivating relatives of the people who died in a place like Neuengamme.'

She did not relent. 'Not Harold, Inspector. He did not talk about the war, or about his part in it. Never. Oh, once, shortly before we were married, he told me where he had been during the war, what his duties had been. I think he did that so that I'd know; so that later on, if it ever came up, I wouldn't be shocked or unprepared. He even told me how it was before he escaped to America, after the Russians arrived in Berlin. It was terrible, he said, but that was all, and he never brought up the subject again.'

'Old friends from Germany, Mrs Oberhauser . . . ?'

'Absolutely none, Inspector. Not in all the years we were married . . . I'm not sure he'd have seen them anyway. As I keep telling you, Inspector, he absolutely refused to consider that part of his life.'

He digressed purposefully in an effort to catch her, and seemed to succeed, when he said, 'How about Kramer?'

The shadow came and went, swiftly. So swiftly in fact Forster wasn't certain he'd seen it, although he had been watching closely.

'What about Kramer, Inspector?' she enquired calmly.

'Visitors, friends, acquaintances; did anyone ever drop by to see Kramer from his war years?'

The smooth features were as bland as before when she shook her head. 'I don't think so, but you see, I really have had very little to do with Kramer. Maybe he had friends I didn't know about. His rooms are off the garage; it's entirely possible he had visitors in the evening. I wouldn't have known, you see.'

Forster tried again, watching more closely this time. 'Maybe Doctor Brown dropped round to see Kramer. Or your husband. Did you know that Doctor Brown's former name was Heinrich Braun, and he was also a Nazi German?'

Again the faintest shadow of uneasiness came and went before the beautiful woman replied. 'No, I didn't know Doctor Brown's name wasn't Brown. As for his past . . .' She lifted lovely shoulders and let them drop.

'Harold and I never really discussed the man; he was just a neighbour, that was all.'

Forster arose smiling. 'Well, it's been very pleasant visiting with you,' he said. 'I'll let you know what I turn up about this letter.' He kept smiling as she escorted him to the door, and only stopped smiling when he slid into the car to drive back to Wilshire Division. Then he said aloud, without any trace of a smile: 'Lady, you are a damned liar.'

By the time he got back an Intelligence report was awaiting him. It had been coded 'top secret' and sent in a sealed envelope up to Captain Hastings's office. Hastings was not back yet from his conference, and his lovely secretary, Virginia, handed Forster the envelope with a solemn, big-eyed look, and an admonition.

'It must be the original and only formula for conjuring up the Devil. I've only seen one really restricted report come through, before, in all the seven years I've worked at Wilshire Division.'

Forster smiled, went back down to his own office, ripped open the envelope, and saw that what he had was the equivalent of an Army Intelligence top-secret report on a German, in this case, on Harold Oberhauser.

It made fascinating reading, but all Forster really wanted to know was the length of time Oberhauser had been in Berlin after Germany's fall, what he had done during that time, and his subsequent moves and behaviour patterns. It was all there, almost day by day. He finally folded the report thinking that the CIA, for all its vaunted specialization in undercover work, could not have done any better than G2 had done.

He was arising after locking his top drawer on the intelligence report, when John Blaine walked in looking hot and tired. He stepped across, dropped two duplicator sheets atop the desk, so fresh they still smelt of the developing fluid, then he loosened his tie, went to his own desk and dropped down back there as he said, 'Hot. Damned hot and sticky up the coast today.'

Forster picked up the two papers, each one being an enlargement of three excellent fingerprints. One of the copies was of an Immigration print-card, the other, with no writing on it to identify its source, was an exact duplicate, and Forster did not need a magnifying glass to make this out.

He said, 'Oberhauser?'

Blaine nodded. 'Yeah. That's where I've been the last half hour, getting the print I brought back blown up and compared. They are the same, so the nut who wouldn't identify himself over the telephone this morning was right, he did see Oberhauser up the coast trying to fix his car.'

'Where did you lift these fresh prints?'

'Right where a mechanic from a nearby

garage took me back and showed me exactly where the car had been when Oberhauser had walked down and got the mechanic to drive back with him to make the repair. On a steel guard-rail. The mechanic showed me precisely where Oberhauser had stood, waiting for the mechanic to make the repair. The car had a broken fuel pump, no big deal, except that cars don't work without functioning fuel pumps.'

Blaine still wasn't comfortable, so he shed his coat. 'I described the guy in the morgue. The mechanic identified Oberhauser. I said I'd send him up a photograph for a positive identification. He said he'd appear in court if we asked it. He also said the car was only a couple of years old, but it was dirty as though it had been used a lot lately.' Blaine smiled for the first time since entering the office. 'It was registered to Oberhauser Industries. The mechanic said he always made a point of memorizing registration slips and licence numbers, just in case some guy stranded like that gave him a bum cheque. The licence number's on the back of the duplicate fingerprint-card. I've already had it put on the wanted list to be sent along to the State Highway Patrol.' Blaine finally began to look a little less warm. He twisted round, pulled a folded newspaper from a coat pocket and tossed it across to Forster's desk. 'Dumas sent that along. I ran into him on his way out, downstairs, he said you asked him to bring that paper in. It's the one Kramer was reading in the park last night.' Blaine, having said all this, lit a cigar, cocked his big feet atop the desk, and eyed Forster, who looked cool and comfortable. 'And what did you accomplish today, my man?'

Reg sat down, kept studying the fingerprints, and related his interlude at the Oberhauser residence. Towards the end of this dissertation, satisfied about the identical composition of the two sets of fingerprints, he unlocked the desk drawer, lifted out the unmarked envelope and tossed it across. 'Read that,' he said, and turned completely around to open the rear-wall window.

As John began reading, Forster's telephone rang. Captain Hastings was back in his office. He wanted to see both Forster and Blaine. As Forster put down the telephone and stood up, picking up the fingerprint cards, he jerked his head. 'Bring that report and let's go. Ben wants a conference.'

Blaine arose slowly. 'This is one hell of a report,' he said, admiringly. 'CIA?'

'Army Intelligence in Germany. Get a move on.'

As they went up the hall, Forster was considering a plan. He did not mention it to Blaine, and even after they were both seated in Captain Hastings's private sanctum, he kept it to himself.

Hastings was as amiable as ever, but his

gaze was hard and uncompromising as he outlined his position. He had been needled at his conference by the mayor, the Police Commissioner, and the City Attorney, for not being able to give them more information than he had available about the Oberhauser case.

Forster knew what was coming and forestalled it by handing over the duplicate fingerprint cards, explaining how John had matched them, and then, finally, by also handing over the Intelligence report on Harold Oberhauser.

Hastings was placated, somewhat anyway, and he was also very interested, but in the end he said, 'I don't mean to lean on you guys, but they raked me over the coals this morning. I know I have no right to demand the impossible but—can you come up with something definite by tomorrow night? That's all the time they gave me.' Hastings smiled a trifle wanly. 'I know what you think of ultimatums. I think the same of them. But we're in a hell of a spot on this Oberhauser affair. At least give me something I can pass along to the Commissioner by tomorrow night, that will get him off my tail for a few days, until you can turn up something hard. Okay?'

Blaine said, 'If the Highway Patrol picks up Oberhauser that ought to bust this thing wide open.'

Hastings's wan smile lingered. 'If,' he said softly. 'If, John.'

Blaine nodded understandingly, and faced Forster. 'Any ideas?'

Forster had one. He hadn't intended to use it yet, but now it appeared he had to, so he said, 'Mrs Oberhauser lied to me today, a couple of times. Also, she gave me a fake letter from some guy named Kaplan in New York purporting to be a threat, at least a *veiled* threat, against her husband. The implication seemed to be that this Kaplan was part of some group that had it in for Nazi concentration camp officers, which is believable.'

Blaine, who had liked the idea all along that Oberhauser could have been trying to drop from sight to avoid being assassinated by vengeful former inmates of Nazi camps, or their surviving descendants, said, 'How do you know it's a fake letter?'

Forster fished the envelope out and handed it over. 'She told me it had arrived in the post yesterday afternoon. Look at the postmark, John. Not the New York postmark, the one stamped on the envelope here in Los Angeles. It's dated today.'

Blaine finished scanning the envelope and handed it to Ben Hastings as he said, 'Okay, so she missed by a day. That's not a big thing.'

Forster agreed. 'No, that's not a big thing, except that plain mail, posted in New York yesterday, can't possibly reach Los Angeles, on the West coast, the very next day.'

John arose to step beside the desk and frowningly re-examine the envelope. Ben Hastings raised his eyes to Forster's face. 'Meaning . . . ?' he said.

'Meaning, that while that letter was post-marked in New York yesterday, and it arrived here today, *plain* mail, *not* air mail, which at the best takes a full three days, someone picked it up in New York and had to bring it with him when he flew out here from New York.'

Blaine and Hastings went back to studying the envelope again, while Reg Forster finally put into words what had been on his mind the last half hour.

'We've got enough discrepancies to bring someone in. The question is, who will it be, Irene Oberhauser, Joseph Kramer, or Henry Brown?'

Hastings gently put down the envelope without even looking at the letter inside it. He did not take up Forster's topic, he instead said, 'Someone's clumsy or careless. He should have known those post-marks wouldn't wash.'

Forster shrugged. 'Be thankful he *was* careless, Ben.'

Hastings nodded, then he said, 'All right; who do you want to haul in?'

Forster did not even hesitate. 'The Irish maid with the handsome smile.'

CHAPTER TEN

ACTION!

Captain Hastings was not astonished, because he was not well enough into the case to know which of the people who had known Harold Oberhauser were considered worthwhile suspects, but John Blaine stared.

'The maid?' he exclaimed. 'We haven't even interrogated her.'

Forster arose, 'Yeah, I know. I also know that the minute we pick up Irene Oberhauser, Kramer or Brown, we'll blow the lid off. Those three I am entirely confident, are hand in glove.'

'But the maid isn't?' said Captain Hastings.

Forster answered judiciously. 'I don't *think* she is. But the main point, Ben, is that she can be picked up in a store, on a warrant of course, and brought in quietly. There wouldn't be any way to do that with any of the others, without them giving the alarm. I may be wrong as hell; the maid may be as involved as the others are. I just have a feeling that she isn't. But in any case, even if she is involved, she's a small fish. She may not even be missed for a few hours, and with any luck at all, when we take her back she may be afraid to tell the others. It's a risk, but I like her over the others to be brought in.'

Blaine had recovered, and as Forster arose and Ben Hastings made a gesture of acquiescence, John led the way back out through Virginia's office to the corridor, and when they were alone, heading back to their office, John finally said, 'I sure hope you're wrong. She's too pretty to be a fink.'

'It won't do you any good, you're married.'

'I wasn't thinking of trying to promote anything, I was just thinking that she's too darned pretty to be—'

'Then go out and make the pick-up yourself,' said Forster, pausing to open their office door. 'Get a warrant in the Justice Court and do the little job yourself. And while you're driving her in, don't forget that the law requires you to apprise her of her rights.'

Blaine was annoyed. 'You don't have to remind me of my duties.'

Forster smiled disarmingly. 'I know that. I was just going to say, as soon as you've advised her, then turn on all your charm, and try to keep her from being frightened. The best way to do that is to get her to trust you. If she can't, or won't, give us some help, we're going to have to risk flushing the lot of them by bringing in Kramer—who would be my second choice.'

Blaine remained standing back by the door. 'Kramer? You couldn't get the time of day out of that gorilla . . . And if I can't catch the maid running errands, you want me to hang around until she does come out, alone?'

Forster nodded. 'Yeah. I'll call your wife, if you're late, and tell her you'll be late for dinner because you're trying to bag an Irish lass with rosy cheeks, lovely grey eyes, and a build like—'

'You call my wife and I'll mop the floor with you,' stated Blaine, and went down the hall adjusting his hastily snugged-up tie.

Hastings called to announce that he had just been contacted by the local Central Intelligence Agency office with the name of the CIA agent who would be dropping round first thing in the morning.

'Peter Blackwell. He's from Washington. They told me that, and I can't figure out whether we're supposed to feel sorry for this spook, or whether we're supposed to be impressed all to hell.'

Forster had no idea, either, and furthermore he did not especially care. But he *did* care about one thing. 'Stall him, Ben. When he shows up in the morning, try and keep his hot little hands off this case, at least until noon.'

Hastings groaned aloud. 'I can't do that. Well, I *shouldn't* do it. Where is John?'

'He just left to waylay the Oberhauser maid.'

Hastings said, 'You'd better come up with something,' and rang off.

Forster seconded that pronouncement to

himself; he had better come up with something. Not because Ben Hastings had said so, but because, sure as hell, now that the police were going after the initiative, it was going to upset the entire nest out there in Westwood. With Oberhauser already running, it shouldn't take a whole lot to scare up the rest of the covey.

The surveillance team covering Henry Brown called in to be put through, and the moment Forster answered, a tough, drawling voice said, 'Our principal and another man, one we have not seen before, but who must have been in the house, have just come out and are now getting into the principal's car. The second man is carrying a flight bag. We will continue surveillance and report in when the principal and his companion reach a destination.'

Forster rang off and, after a moment of wonder, snapped his fingers. The man who had recently arrived from New York! The man who had brought the fake letter to Irene Oberhauser! He was the only person, so far, who was not a local resident.

Of course, people carrying flight bags in Los Angeles were a penny a dozen.

Forster, acceding to a hunch, called the surveillance team back and ascertained that they were still following Henry Brown and his unknown subject. When he was told they were approaching the carriageway leading to Grand

Central Airport, Forster's hunch, having been vindicated, prompted him to say, 'After he's left his companion at the airport, get all the information you can on the stranger flying out of Los Angeles. Name, destination, where he came from, even his vitals, if you can get them.'

That same tough-sounding, drawling voice said, 'We can pick him up, if you'd like,' and Forster's answer was quick and incisive.

'No. But let me know the minute his aircraft is on its way.'

This time, as Forster settled back, he began to feel that the tempo was picking up; that, finally, the cat-and-mouse phase of the Oberhauser affair was beginning to reverse itself, that the offensive was passing to Homicide Division.

Hastings called to ask if Forster had sent anyone out to Oberhauser Industries to verify that the car Harold Oberhauser had fled in, had indeed come from there. Forster's reply was negative, and his reason was elemental. 'One word out there that the police know Oberhauser has a company car, and any cohorts he might have out there will also know how close we are to Oberhauser, not to mention that they will realize the police know the corpse at the morgue is not Harold Oberhauser.'

Hastings said no more, which allowed Forster to contact the surveillance team at the airport, and ascertain that they were now keeping both Brown and his unidentified companion in sight in the lounge. For the time being there was no more to be learned from this source, so Forster went next door for a cup of coffee, and when he returned to the office, John Blaine was there—alone.

'The maid is gone,' he reported.

Forster stopped dead still in the doorway, entirely unprepared for this. 'Gone?' he repeated, and began moving towards his desk, coffee cup in hand.

'I contacted the team assigned to Mrs Oberhauser, who hadn't left the house, they told me, but while we were talking, Mrs Oberhauser came out, got into a car and left. The team pulled out too. So I went over there to find the maid. She wasn't there. No one was there. The maid's room in the back of the house was cleaned out. I could see the open closet from a rear window, and a cleaned out dresser. There was—'

'Kramer was gone too?' asked Forster.

'I didn't look in his rooms off the garage, but if his surveillance men are out there, you could—'

'In a minute,' said Forster. 'How in the hell could the maid have slipped out without being seen, John? Hell's bells, we've got two teams out there.'

'If she did it last night,' stated Blaine, 'it's quite possible. *She* wasn't under surveillance.

She could have packed her bag and—'

Forster suddenly started, then lunged for the telephone. He called the team at the airport breathlessly to enquire whether Henry Brown and his companion were still in the lounge, and was informed by transceiver that the aircraft for which the stranger had evidently been waiting, was now in process of loading. Forster snapped an order. 'Grab Brown's companion. Try and do it without Brown seeing you make the apprehension, but grab him and hustle him down here as quickly as you can.'

Blaine was staring at Forster. When the telephone had been replaced Blaine said, 'What the hell was that all about?'

'You said the maid could have packed her bag. Henry Brown is with someone his surveillance team has not seen before, who came out of the house with Brown a little while ago, and went to the airport—carrying a flight bag.'

'So.'

'So—it's got to be the maid.'

John continued to stare. 'Why does it have to be the maid, Reg? There's still another unknown principal wandering around, somewhere. The guy who flew in from New York City with the fake letter for Irene Oberhauser.'

Forster's telephone rang. This time the call was from the surveillance team following Irene

Oberhauser. Their principal had just picked up another woman, a rather young, dowdy-looking woman, at a local employment agency. The dowdy woman had two suitcases with her. Mrs Oberhauser was now driving back in the general direction of her residence.

Forster said, 'One of you guys go back to the employment agency, find out everything you can about the girl, and get back to me with what you get.' He then put aside the telephone and looked searchingly at John Blaine. 'Mrs Oberhauser just hired another maid.'

Blaine looked more baffled than interested. 'Let's go back—if this guy you yanked off the aeroplane isn't the maid—then what?'

'Then I'm wrong,' stated Forster, succinctly. 'But that's happened before, and in any case, if this person can be brought in without Henry Brown's knowledge, we'll still have someone who may be able to help the investigation. At the worst, he might be—'

'The guy who brought the fake letter from New York,' stated John, beginning to see a glimmer of light through the tunnel of his doubts. 'I wish to hell we could get our hands on something solid, for a change. This mess is like trying to put your thumb on quicksilver. I'll take a nice, tidy, everyday murder based on hatred or jealousy or greed, any day of the week.'

Blaine went next door for coffee, and the team at the airport called in to say they had very quietly removed the passenger from the aeroplane, after Henry Brown had shaken hands with his companion in the airport lounge, and had gone back out to his car to depart. They were now on their way to Wilshire Division.

Forster said, 'Is your principal a man or a woman?'

That seemed to startle the tough-drawling detective. For a moment he said nothing, then his answer came back. 'Man, Inspector ... Wait a minute ... Inspector? It's a woman dressed as a man, with dark glasses and face hair. I wouldn't have believed it.'

Forster arose and went to stand looking out the rear-wall window, some of the doorknobs in his stomach atrophying. When John walked in Reg turned. 'About once a year the fates let me win one; that guy they picked up at the airport is a woman. I just talked to the surveillance team.'

Blaine's face brightened with a broad smile of relief. 'You had me worried for a while,' he said, sitting down at the desk. 'I could see our heads getting lopped off by a Board of Inquiry for interfering with the freedom of a citizen.'

The team following Mrs Oberhauser called in to report that their principal had gone directly home from the employment agency, and was there now. They also had a report on the dowdy woman Mrs Oberhauser had picked up. She had only applied for domestic work the previous day, giving the name of Eilene Hamstead, and giving as her preference some domicile in the Westwood area, and, uniquely enough, Mrs Oberhauser, of Westwood, had called in for a domestic only an hour later. As far as the employment agency was concerned, it was a perfect match. They had collected their fee and closed their files on this particular placement.

Forster said, 'Good work. You can come on in now. We'll take it up again in the morning.' He leaned far back and blew out a big, rough sigh, then he winked at John and said, 'We're moving, finally. We're beginning to roll.'

CHAPTER ELEVEN

THE FIRST BREAKTHROUGH

There was no doubt about the identity of the maid, despite her excellent disguise as a man. Both Blaine and Forster recognized her the moment she was brought through the doorway.

Forster sent the accompanying detectives away with the flight bag, then waited until Blaine, who had brought up a chair for the maid, had returned to his desk, before speaking to the grey-eyed woman whose infectious smile had so impressed both the detectives on their previous meeting. This time, the woman was not smiling. She was stonily impassive, and seemed to be quite relaxed, quite composed, which was a little unusual—unless of course she was nowhere nearly as fresh and uncomplicated as Forster and Blaine had thought she would be. Or unless she was a consummate actress.

The initial few moments were a little awkward, then Forster said, 'You almost made it,' and the pretty girl did not drop her eyes as she answered. 'Almost doesn't count, does it?'

Blaine and Forster exchanged a look. She was young, very attractive, and apparently cynically knowledgeable. It was a little disillusioning for them both; they were not romanticists—no one is who has been a policeman for any length of time—but they could still hope a little, which is exactly what they had both been doing; hoping she would come out of this, some plausible way.

She wasn't going to, though.

Forster asked where she had been going, and she answered candidly. 'New York. The ticket is still in my pocket.' Then, without raising her voice she said, 'Do you have a warrant for me?'

Blaine, in whom the hope was dying hardest, sighed and shook his head. 'Yes, lady, we have a warrant for your arrest.'

She flicked a look at Blaine, then did as Irene Oberhauser had done, concentrated her full attention upon Reg Forster. 'I'm entitled to a lawyer.'

Forster conceded this point. 'You are. What name did they book you under when they brought you in, downstairs?'

'Peggy Bryan.'

'Is that your real name?'

'Can you think of any reason why it shouldn't be my real name, Inspector?'

Forster very gently inclined his head. 'One reason, Peggy: Murder.' When she accepted this with no change, Forster decided to try shock. He said, 'You'll have company—Eilene Hamstead.'

The shock showed, suddenly and unmistakably. Then Peggy Bryan calmly said, 'Who is Eilene Hamstead?' and Forster, instead of answering, asked if she'd like a cup of coffee, and she accepted the offer, but the moment John Blaine went out of the room to accommodate her, she said, 'Inspector Forster, you're a policeman, and this is California, and I have just as many rights as you have, and if I'm in trouble with the law, I have *more* rights. You have charged me, now I'm entitled to a lawyer, and unless it's a capital crime, I'm eligible for freedom under bail.'

Forster listened, folded his hands together atop the desk, and studied the pretty girl for a while before saying anything at all. Eventually, he tried to shock her again. As before, he succeeded, but with greater and unexpected results this second time.

'You'll get your rights,' he told her, speaking quietly. He smiled. 'You're fairly well informed about California law, too. Except for one thing. Murder is a capital crime, and a direct charge under the first degree, is not ordinarily subject to bail.'

'First degree!' she exclaimed. '*I* didn't kill him.'

'Kill who?'

'Harold Oberhauser. That's who you're talking—'

'No one killed Harold Oberhauser and you know it. But someone killed his impersonator, and you know about that, too.'

She checked her readied exclamation and gazed at Forster, with her mouth ajar. He had the advantage, and he kept it by pressing on.

'Irene Oberhauser knew, so did Kramer and Doctor Brown. As for the capital crime—we're not charging you with murder, we've got another capital crime, one that is on the *national* books—it's called espionage, and to a lot of Americans it's much more serious than a local charge of murder, or complicity in a murder. Espionage carries a maximum prison term of—'

Peggy Bryan suddenly said, 'You can't connect me with anything subversive, Inspector. All I ever did was carry messages.' When John Blaine opened the door, carrying three cups of coffee, the girl started in her chair, swiftly turned, saw who was entering, then sank limply back and faced Forster again.

He did not allow the agitation any time to abate. 'Carried messages,' he said, to focus her recaptured attention on what they had been discussing prior to Blaine's return. 'How did Eilene Hamstead get the letter to Mrs Oberhauser, which Eilene brought from New York day before yesterday?'

But the girl had used that split moment of John's return, to recover. She had damned herself, but now she had recovered, so all she said was, 'Who is Eilene Hamstead?' and Forster, in the act of reaching for the telephone, was interrupted, this time by a detective named Bruner, who had been one of the men who had apprehended the girl at the airport. Without looking at the girl, Bruner brought over a typewritten page, which he placed before Forster, then he dropped a small, brown envelope beside the report, and said, 'We sent the original to cryptology,' and pointed to a paragraph in the typed report. 'It was wadded up inside a perfume vial and hidden inside the locking mechanism of the valise's lock. It showed up in x-ray.' He shot John a glance, over the girl's head, then said, 'The rest of the bag's contents are inventoried there, Inspector, at the bottom of the page. Cryptology will be calling you on the note . . . Anything else?'

There wasn't, so Forster sent the man away,

and looked steadily at Peggy Bryan without reading the report, and without speaking for a long time. The girl was losing her stolid look, but she was tough and Forster had guessed as much. He tasted the coffee, set the cup aside, and finally, with the silence drawing taut, looked down at the report.

The girl spoke. 'This amounts to arbitrary seizure, and a denial of my rights. I want to contact a lawyer.'

Forster raised hard, stone-steady eyes. 'You're in trouble,' he said softly, 'and we are going to hold you for the CIA. Peggy, we're simple city detectives. Espionage isn't our bag. There is a CIA office here in Los Angeles, and there's an agent named Blackwell on his way out to visit us, to arrive in the morning. My guess is that you'll be taken back to Washington with him, as a federal prisoner . . . Lawyer? They'll get you one.' Forster chose his words carefully; he wanted to imply that 'they' were now going to take her over, and civilian due-process would no longer apply. 'Now listen to me; you can deny the charges until you're blue in the face. It won't change a darned thing. Believe me, or not, as you please, but if I were in your boots, I think I'd opt for complicity here in California, and maybe come out of this all in one piece, and probably even free, rather than go through a drawn-out federal investigation, and an even longer federal court trial, with a very good chance of being found guilty of espionage, and end up with a ten-to-twenty-year prison sentence . . . Peggy?'

She said, 'Complicity . . . ?'and Forster's heart skipped a beat. He had made his point!

'Complicity means knowledge of, or involvement in, the commission of a crime. In this instance, the crime will be the murder of John Doe—the man down at the coroner's place, who looked exactly like Harold Oberhauser.'

She drank some coffee, and kept watching Forster's face over the rim of the cup. As she lowered the cup, she also lowered her eyes, in quiet thought, for a long moment, during which Blaine and Forster exchanged a fleeting look, then, when she raised her eyes, Forster spoke again. 'If we charge you locally, first, that charge will take precedence.'

'The CIA can't take me back to Washington, then?'

No. Not without some kind of executive, judicial tug-of-war with us, out here, and the CIA doesn't very often go into court, like that.' Forster leaned on the desk. 'If you didn't shoot that man at the morgue, then you'll be—'

'Shoot him,' she suddenly exclaimed. 'I didn't even *know* him.' She paused for breath, then spoke again in the same gusty way. 'They didn't tell me he wasn't Mr Oberhauser. Not until this morning when Doctor Brown gave me the clothes I have on now. All I knew, was that last night Mrs Oberhauser gave me the capsule to hide in the flight bag's specially made lock, with orders to wait until midnight, then go with Joseph Kramer through the back gardens over to Doctor Brown's house. Doctor Brown completed the disguise, and took me to the airport. He told me that wasn't Mr Oberhauser when I said I was afraid; that Mr Oberhauser had always been nice to me; that I would deliver the message in New York, then I was going to leave the Organization. Doctor Brown agreed that if I felt this way, I should leave—but at the airport he told me to be sure and go directly to my contact in New York City—and that frightened me ... It sounded too much like Doctor Brown was going to telephone New York about me. When the detectives took me off the aeroplane, I was petrified; I thought, at first, they were some of the Organization men, and Doctor Brown had decided not to wait until I reached New York ... Inspector, I'm telling you the truth. I didn't know that wasn't Harold Oberhauser, and I have no idea who killed him.'

Reg listened, reached for his coffee, and glanced over where John Blaine, top-desk drawer open, out of the girl's sight, was keeping one hand out of sight in the drawer, then Forster finished his coffee.

He'd had no idea how terrified the girl really was, and he'd only had a vague, unsupported hunch, about her real connection with something he suspected existed, but until just now, could not have defined, nor proved existed.

Peggy Bryan was a windfall. If she hadn't been terrified, if that terror hadn't finally broken through her tough and knowledgeable earlier attitude, Forster and Blaine would have been in a precarious position. He accepted his turn of good fortune philosophically; after all, they'd had nothing but bad luck up until now, so they were certainly entitled to a *little* good luck.

Forster was convinced that his jarring statements to the girl had completed the shattering of her composure, which had begun the moment Henry Brown had aroused her suspicions, but he took no credit; he wasn't interested in that, he was interested in effecting a final and total breakthrough, and he did not have much time. Only until tomorrow morning.

He said, 'Peggy, we'll need a witnessed and notarized statement about the Organization, and about your connection with it.'

She said, 'Inspector, if I give you that, can you guarantee my safety? Will a statement by me amount to being a witness for the State?'

John Blaine blinked at the girl, evidently surprised at her understanding of the law. He still had his hand out of sight in the desk-drawer, where the monitoring device was silently taping everything that was being said.

Forster's answer was typical of any detective in his position. 'That'll be up to the prosecuting attorney. In most cases, turning state's evidence amounts to being a friendly witness, and at the court's discretion, entitles you to lenient consideration. If you'd like, I'll call the City Attorney right now, and—'

The girl interrupted. 'That's not what I'm worried about. They'll try to kill me, Inspector. I have to know you'll protect me. Look; I'm *sure* Doctor Brown would have told the Organization to meet me at the airport in New York . . . I was trying to figure a way to leave the aeroplane before it landed back there, when your detectives came after me just before the aeroplane left Los Angeles. Inspector, I need a guarantee.'

Her last sentence rang with desperation. Forster could guarantee her safety as long as she was in custody *in Los Angeles*. He gave her that promise, and from the corner of his eye saw the look John Blaine was putting on him. John knew the limitations as well as Reg did. But Reg had something else in mind; even if he had to go on annual leave to do it, and dissociate himself from the Department while he did it, he was going to see that, in exchange for her full co-operation, she would not be endangered.

'You've got to trust someone,' he told her, and smiled. 'You're not going to be able to do much by yourself. We'll do everything that can be done to keep you safe.'

She did not return his smile, but she seemed to loosen slightly in the chair, and Forster reached for the telephone to summons Captain Hastings, and a stenographer.

CHAPTER TWELVE

MORE FACTS EMERGE

Ben Hastings would not permit a statement to be taken until the girl had legal counsel present, and because the Department could not recommend a lawyer, and Peggy Bryan did not know any attorneys in Los Angeles, John Blaine resolved the problem by sitting the girl at his desk with a weighty city directory before her. In the end, she demonstrated that unique perception again by telephoning the Los Angeles Legal Aid Council for a name, and then contacted a lawyer named Millstein, who said he would be right over.

Millstein arrived, and between his beard and long hair, and his generally unkempt appearance, got a cold, sceptical stare from the policemen, as well as from the police matron required by law to be present during the interrogation of female prisoners.

But looks could be deceiving. As it turned out, Millstein was a deep-dyed Establishment

105

man. When the interrogation finally began, and his 'client' told of being sent to California as a courier, ostensibly to act the part of a domestic in search of work on the West Coast, and explained that messages were sent this way because the Organization on the East Coast made a fetish of acting as though its members were under constant surveillance, Millstein did not object, as most lawyers would have done, on the grounds that the girl was incriminating herself.

In fact, Millstein seemed engrossed in what his client was saying; so engrossed, in fact, that he did not even interrupt to warn her against self-incrimination. But afterwards, when Peggy had been taken away by the matron, to be incarcerated, Millstein flapped his arms at the detectives and said, 'It's unbelievable. I've never run into anything like this before.' Then he showed that he had not been entirely derelict, by saying, 'But of course, she's such a minor cog, she can't possibly come out of this with a serious sentence.'

The entire interrogation required two full hours, and all the detectives had actually learned was that Peggy Bryan, like her replacement at the Oberhauser residence, Eilene Hamstead, had been a courier, that the Organization had other couriers, some men, some women; that Harold Oberhauser had evidently been the West Coast executive of the Organization; that he had, over the past half dozen or so years built up a small, tight, very dedicated and sophisticated West Coast cell of the Organization.

Of the Organization itself, she knew little. Its purpose, she said, was to bring power down to the working people, to advocate an equitable distribution of the wealth, and to organize an underground force which could come to the aid of the oppressed. Even Millstein rolled up his eyes over this. 'I've met hundreds of them,' he told the detectives. 'Mostly, about her age, too. It doesn't seem to occur to them that they are being used; they don't even question the fact that their leaders are more autocratic, more capitalistic, than the purported capitalists.'

But Ben Hastings was more sceptical. 'If that's all it is, another tiresome communist conspiracy—I wish someone would explain to me why it's so topheavy with former Nazi Germans.'

Reg Forster had the answer to that. 'To start with, Ben, you have to go back almost thirty years. Kramer, the former German soldier, went all the way up to Moscow with the *Wehrmacht,* and was captured there by the Soviets. His story was that he escaped back to the West by pretending to be a German who was repatriatable. Harold Oberhauser was still in Berlin when the Soviets took the place. Henry Brown was also still at his post when the Russians arrived. Now then—if you'd studied their backgrounds as well as I have, you'd notice one similarity. Maybe they didn't know one another in those days, but all three of them were swallowed up in the vacuum that prevailed throughout Russian-occupied Germany immediately after the war. We don't know what happened to them during that time, but we *do* know they were in Soviet custody for a fairly long time ... Then, they turned up over here, separately, at different intervals in time, seeking US citizenship. There were sponsors—in Oberhauser's case, Doctor Henry Brown, the least objectionable to the Allies because he'd been a scientist, already well settled in America, respectable as all hell.

'It followed a pattern, Ben. First, the best of the lot was sent over to become U.S. citizens and to become settled—in the way Brown did—as an eminent physicist, an instructor. Then, a few years later, this established person sponsors one like Oberhauser, who, during the same intervening years, has lived a model life in Germany. So on, right down the line until the former prisoner-of-war, Kramer, could also get over here. But Kramer was not a prisoner of the Soviets for very long. I'll bet a year's salary on that. He was recruited exactly as Brown and Oberhauser, and the Lord only knows how many others, were recruited.'

Forster turned his attention upon the lawyer. 'Mr Millstein, maybe it's hack to you, and I can understand how you feel, but for one thing: Murder.'

The telephone rang, interrupting Forster. He picked it up, said his name, listened briefly, then offered the instrument to Captain Hastings, and as the bureau chief was occupied with his call, Forster turned back to Millstein again.

'We've got enough from Peggy Ryan to give the FBI for a roundup of subversives, or whatever they are, back on the East Coast, but all this doesn't help LAPD, does it? I mean— we're cops, not spy-catchers. I particularly want a murderer. His purpose for committing murder interests me, of course, but before that, I want him, and it looks now as though we're really not a lot closer, doesn't it?'

Millstein arose shrugging narrow shoulders. 'I got faith,' he said, smiling. 'I got faith in LAPD, Inspector.' He made the V peace signal, and left the office, and just before closing the door, Millstein said he'd be back in the afternoon to see his client.

The moment the door closed, Hastings put down the telephone. With a sigh he said, 'They got a fix on the corpse. I won't even attempt to pronounce his name. It'll be along with the Intelligence report, from Washington. He's a Pole, a former Polish seaman. He was captured in some kind of petty-ante naval confrontation between the Polish merchant marine and some Soviet trawlers about six years ago, was reported missing at sea and was never heard of again. And now he turns up on a slab in the coroner's cold-room looking exactly like a guy named Oberhauser.'

'Who also,' said John Blaine, 'had some kind of unexplained sojourn among the Soviets.'

Forster threw up his hands. 'The murderer,' he exclaimed. 'Damn it all, we're supposed to be concerned with a murderer.' He dropped his hands and arose to step back by the window. 'I think we'd better round up the lot, now. Surely one of them will know something about the murder.'

Blaine spoke up. 'That'll blow the case for us, Reg.'

Forster's retort was brusque. 'It's already blown, John. At least it will be the minute that aeroplane lands in New York, and the girl isn't on it. If Brown called back there, the Organization would have its reception committee on hand. When she doesn't show up, they're going to call Brown back—and that ought to spook hell out of them all. I think we'd ought to bring them in, but especially Brown—*before* he learns that the girl didn't disembark at New York, and blows the whistle.'

Captain Hastings, sitting slouched, with one hand partially supporting his head while he listened, finally shoved up out of the chair and nodded at Forster. 'You're right. I'll be in my office if you need me, or if you turn up anything.' He had started for the door when the telephone stopped him. He waited while Forster answered, then, as Forster listened, and looked from Blaine to Hastings, the captain sighed and leaned on the wall, patiently waiting.

When Forster rang off he looked both pleased and quizzical. 'The Highway Patrol's got Oberhauser's car. It was found abandoned on the beach just north of Santa Barbara.' Forster went to his desk and eased down upon a corner of it before continuing to speak. 'And there were several reports to the Coast Guard station up there about a seaplane flying along the coast lower than the law allows. No markings of any kind on the aircraft. The Coast Guard cleared this through the Highway Patrol in case the aircraft was in trouble, but there's been no report of such an aircraft landing anywhere between Santa Barbara and Ventura. However, a commercial fisherman reported to the Patrol that a seaplane landed not very far from where Oberhauser's abandoned car was found.'

Hastings straightened up and put a hand on the doorknob. 'Exit Harold Oberhauser. This Organization must be pretty high up in the chips; even to lease a seaplane costs heaps.' He nodded at Blaine and Forster, and went out into the corridor. 'Lots of luck,' were his last words, before closing the door.

Blaine said, 'Seaplanes, secret agents, coded

messages,' and threw up his arms. 'You want me to go out and bag the lot and bring them back for questioning?'

Forster said, 'No; I want you to go get a fistful of John Doe warrants for arrest and meet me downstairs at the car, and we'll *both* go bag the lot.'

Blaine arose, closed his top-desk drawer, and departed. Forster picked up the report on the contents of Peggy Ryan's flight bag, which he'd only glanced at earlier, and got thwarted by the ringing telephone. It was the cryptologist attached to Special Operations Squad, downstairs.

The message found in the flight bag of Peggy Ryan had been deciphered without too much difficulty, the cryptologist reported. Its message, however, did not appear to make much sense, unless of course the recipient knew what the terms meant. It said simply: 'Let Arcana seek, the storm is over.'

Forster thanked the cryptologist, rang off, arose from the desk and sauntered down to the large lobby, and from there outside into the continuing heat. He had no idea who 'Arcana' was, although he thought it had to be someone, or some *thing*, involved one way or another in a hunt for Harold Oberhauser, but he was reasonably sure that 'the storm is over' referred to the fake death of Oberhauser, who had been a *Sturm*bannfuhrer. At least this was Forster's surmise, while he stood beside the car awaiting Blaine, and when John eventually came up, stating that he had the warrants, Forster used him as a sounding-board for the decoded message, and John, driving the car out of the parking area, agreed that Forster's guess was as good as any, then John concentrated on heading for the Westwood area, in a cheerful mood.

Forster did not call for a uniformed back-up, but about the time they were leaving the arterial throughway and heading towards the neighbourhood of the Oberhauser residence, he informed Communications that the surveillance teams should close in, and watch Forster and Blaine; if there was any sign of trouble, they were to move in and lend support.

But Forster expected no difficulty. Irene Oberhauser, in particular, was not a person Forster could believe was likely to be dangerous. Kramer, of course, was a different matter, but as they drove along he and John discussed Kramer. They would arrest Irene first, then go together out, back to Kramer's quarters, and try to effect a surprise.

Blaine said, 'Yeah. An *armed* surprise.'

Doctor Brown was at home. They were certain of this as they cruised past his residence, and saw his car in the driveway, on their way farther along, to the Oberhauser residence.

John parked out front, turned to look all

around before alighting, and when he saw none of the surveillance men he shoved open the car door with a grunt and a growl. 'You never see a cop when you need one.'

They strolled towards the invitingly shaded large patio looking more than ever like a pair of big, rumpled and dispirited St Bernard dogs. Forster looked off in the direction of the garage, and the lower end of the patio before knocking, half expecting Kramer silently to materialize as he had done once before. But there was no one in sight; in fact, there was an air of siesta-like late-day drowsiness over the entire neighbourhood, as though, when the heat bore down, everyone sought a cool, shadowy place to sleep.

Then Forster knocked, and the door was opened by a girl with a sprinkling of freckles across the bridge of her nose, a very severely plain and prim method of drawing her mouse-coloured hair straight back into a bun, and whose round, rather stolid-appearing face, turned towards the detectives, showed nothing at all.

Forster asked for Mrs Oberhauser and was admitted. The moment John Blaine was inside, he eased the door closed at his back, showed the maid his ID folder, then pointed to an antique ladderback chair in the entry-hall as he said, 'Sit down there, please, and don't make any noise. Just *sit*!'

CHAPTER THIRTEEN

CHAOS!

Statuesque Irene Oberhauser appeared in the entry-way opening, looking quizzically regal. The moment she recognized her callers, she came forward, brows arched in silent enquiry. Very slowly she turned towards the girl in the chair, looking slightly annoyed and slightly puzzled. Forster could follow almost every thought that crossed the handsome woman's mind, right up until he spoke, then he saw the mask settle over her face.

He said, 'Mrs Oberhauser, we have a warrant for your arrest, along with warrants for the arrest of Brown, Kramer, and this girl, Eilene Hamstead.'

The tall woman raised her hands, clasping them together. Otherwise, she made no sign that she had been either upset by Forster, or surprised by his announcement.

She worked a large ruby ring round the finger on her left hand, with the fingers of her right hand, and finally she said, 'On what grounds, Inspector?'

'For being an accessory to murder, Mrs Oberhauser.'

The beautiful woman smiled, and to Forster it looked as though she were immensely

115

relieved. 'I didn't murder anyone, that's ridiculous.'

'No one has accused you of murdering anyone,' replied Forster. 'I said for being an *accessory*.'

'Does that mean I supplied the gun, or something like that?'

Forster looked at the seated maid, whose plain, round face was lifted towards him. Then he looked back at the beautiful woman and gave his answer. 'Your lawyer can supply you with the interpretation of being an accessory, Mrs Oberhauser. All Inspector Blaine and I are here to do is—'

There was a stunning sound, and a subsequent reverberation, outside, as though something quite heavy had fallen against the front wall. John Blaine whirled towards the door, reaching for the latch with one hand while he reached under his coat with the other hand. As he wrenched the door open, a burly man dropped halfway across the patio, rolled into plain view of the people in the entry-way, and a second large man, jumping off the patio to the left, saw Blaine and yelped at him.

'Feller's got a gun!'

That was all the man had time to say before Blaine saw the spurt of shattered cement where a bullet had struck within inches of the crouching, weaving detective out there.

Forster called. 'John! Get away from the door!' The moment Blaine stepped back,

Forster shoved past him, giving an order as he moved ahead. 'Keep these two women under guard and lock this door from the inside.'

Forster dived headlong through the opening, landed beyond the bricked walk of the patio upon the grass, and rolled in the direction of the retreating detective. The other officer had not moved since he'd fallen.

Forster heard the peculiar little whistling grunt of a gun being fired with a silencer, before he could stop rolling. He did not see Kramer. In fact, he never did see him, but each time he heard that whistling grunt, he rolled some more, until he was hidden by a mass of rose bushes planted in the form of a hedge, which divided the front garden of the Oberhauser residence from the farther-back macadamized driveway, and the rear garden.

The other detective, already down on one knee nearby, did not take his eyes off the corner of the house as he said, 'That son of a bitch came out of nowhere, just as we were approaching the house. How in the hell did he know—?' The detective had to drop flat when the whistling grunt came again, three times in rapid succession. As the detective turned and saw Reg Forster looking at him, he said, 'We've got to get help for Brady. I heard the slug hit, it sounded like meat tearing.'

Forster's comment was pithy. 'You stick your head up and you'll *both* need help.' He wiggled half around, found a place where it was possible to peer through the rose bushes, scanned the yonder garage-area, then pulled back and got up on to one knee. 'He's got to be around the far south corner of the house. Between there and his quarters, which are at the far end of the garage. I'm going to try and get around the house from the north end. You keep him occupied, if you can.'

From out front, on the far side of Forster's and Blaine's car, a man whistled. Forster twisted, then waved off the other two surveillance men out there. He had his service revolver in his right hand, had his left hand on the ground to push off with, and when he was ready to sprint, he said, 'Open up on the corner of the house and pin him down until I can get out of sight.'

The detective behind Forster raised his gun and fired. It made a stunning sound in the deadly silence; until that moment the only weapon to be fired was the one with the silencer. Now, as the detective fired three times, rapidly and systematically, as Reg Forster sprinted for the upper corner of the house, the gunshot reverberations quivered in the still air, sending off tumultuous echoes.

Forster had no difficulty reaching the corner of the house. He paused there catching his breath, then, when one of those officers on the far side of the parked car raised up to look around, Forster shook a balled fist, and the man dropped down again.

He started down the far side of the house, grotesquely overwhelmed by the perfume of flowers as he went to kill. At the far end of the north wall he looked around, saw nothing, heard nothing, and stepped beside a massive, low and flourishing acacia tree, at the precise moment another man slipped around the southern section of the house, backing very carefully, and holding a gun low in one hand, holding to the house-wall with the other hand as he acted out a silent retreat.

There was not a sound as Reg Forster raised his gun, waiting with both arms extended, using the acacia's rough, solid bole for its steadying effect, and when the shadowy figure emerging into the back garden was finally completely cut off from the garden out front, and dropped his head to examine the gun in his hand, Forster called him.

'Drop the gun and freeze where you are!'

The man dropped the gun, but he dropped with it. He had a bad handicap; he did not know where Forster's command had come from, so, instead of being able to fire, as he was ready to do, now, gun up, he had to waste moments looking for a target.

Forster pressed the bulk of his body back around the tree and spoke one more time, and the man on the ground fired instantly; high and wide, but he fired.

Forster squeezed off one round at a range, and at a prone and stationary target, he could hardly miss. Impact jerked the bullet-shocked man half up off the ground before he dropped the gun, and wilted beside it.

The echo was still audible while Forster remained over by the acacia tree. Somewhere in the near distance a black-and-white cruiser, travelling in Alert Three with siren screaming, completed the destruction of the suburban silence and serenity which had originally been shattered by the muzzleblast of police weapons.

From the side of the house where Forster had made his way round back, a man called softly.

'Where is he; you got him in sight, back there?'

Forster turned his head. It was that same gung-ho type from out by the car who'd kept sticking his head up. He had his service revolver in his fist. Forster lowered his arms. 'Yeah, I got him in sight. He's face down over by a flowerbed near the lower end of the house.' As the detective started to move away, Forster called him back. 'Listen; go inside and see if my partner's all right. He's got two female prisoners in there. Sing out, and be careful.'

The detective turned back, nodding his head, and with the cruiser's siren sounding steadily closer, Forster left the acacia tree. Unless there were more than one of them with guns, the excitement was over.

The handgun with the silencer on it lay half in the grass a dozen yards from the downed man. Forster stepped over it, never taking his eyes off the man on the pavement. But he had no illusions. He had aimed to kill, and he was one of the best qualifiers on the police pistol range.

The man was dead, that much Forster ascertained from fifteen feet away. From ten feet, then five feet, the effect of Forster's one bullet only showed up more disconcertingly; it had ploughed into the dead man's chest from right to left, as he'd had his right arm raised a little to fire.

Blaine came to the rear door, looked out, then turned as someone inside the house called to him. He hesitated, then reluctantly turned back. The siren was silent now, the cruiser was at kerbside, a red light and an amber light revolving atop its roof. The uniformed men were inside the house, briefly, along with three other detectives. One of the uniformed men walked around into the garden, gun in hand but held low. He called softly to let Forster know he was approaching, then spoke as he came up and halted, gazing at the dead man. 'Ambulance on the way. This the guy who shot the detective?'

Forster put up his weapon and draped the jacket to cover it, on his belt. 'Yeah. How's the detective?'

'Not too bad,' stated the officer.

121

'Concussion from his fall on those patio bricks, I think. Otherwise, the bullet grazed his jaw and stunned him.' The officer leaned. 'You know this guy?'

'Yeah, I know him. His name is Brown. He's a physics instructor at UCLA.' Forster pointed. 'Don't touch that gun.' He turned back as the rear door opened again and John Blaine emerged. Blaine walked over, looked, looked harder, then frowned as his gaze ranged farther along, over in the direction of the double garage, and the quarters on the far side of it.

Forster walked away saying, 'Let's go. If he's in there, he's sure as hell not going to be surprised now.' As he stepped past the uniformed officer he spoke from the side of his mouth. 'You fellows give us support. There may be another one on the far side of the garage.'

The uniformed officer raised his face, looked southward, looked at Forster and Blaine, then turned hurriedly to rush inside the house.

Blaine, studying the garage-area, quietly said, 'You got any idea how this started?'

Forster shook his head, not too interested. He was trying to guess whether Kramer was inside, down there on the far side of the garage, waiting, perhaps with a gun in his hand.

Blaine, still speaking quietly, spoke again.

'You remember how she twisted her hands together when you told her we had a warrant for her?'

Forster turned, sensing something. 'Yeah.'

Blaine reached into his pocket left-handed, withdrew a large ruby ring and held it up. 'You push the damned stone and it transmits a bleep to the wristwatch someone was wearing. Doctor Brown, for instance.'

Forster stared. 'She told you that?'

'Yeah. When I watched her doing it and took the ring off her finger. It was their May Day signal. They were only to use it if they were in complete danger, and needed help immediately.' Blaine dropped the ruby ring back into his pocket, and without taking his eyes off the garage, said, 'If he's down there, why didn't he answer the May Day call like Brown did? Reg, I don't think he's there.'

They moved ahead. Once clear of the house Reg saw uniformed men fanning out. It looked like a whole squad of them, and they had shotguns. If Kramer came out shooting, now, he wasn't going to get off more than one shot.

But he didn't come out.

Forster and Blaine got down the far rear wall of the garage, saw the open window in the living quarters down there, and Forster called for Kramer to come out. Nothing happened. He called again, louder this time, and still nothing happened. He then got beneath the window, raised his revolver, cocked it, came up

123

fast and shoved the gun past a pair of flimsy curtains.

The room was empty.

Blaine went round front, motioned the uniformed officers in closer, then, with one savage kick, half tore the closed door off its hinges. Kramer was not inside. They swarmed in while Forster, at the back window, waited, ready to kill again, but when the bathroom and all the closets had been ransacked without turning up anyone, John Blaine stepped over and said, 'Gone, sure as hell. Now what do we do?'

Forster put up his gun for the second time and turned as masculine voices in the rear garden distracted him. Four men were lifting the corpse of Doctor Henry Brown on to a wheeled stretcher after two other men had finished photographing the body. As Forster watched, someone, using a pencil down the barrel, lifted the silencered revolver.

Forster turned back. 'Let's get the women loaded and head for Wilshire Division.' He looked at John. 'I don't know what the hell happened, John, but I've got a feeling we blew it. Let's go.'

CHAPTER FOURTEEN

THE AFTERMATH OF VIOLENCE

Irene Oberhauser was ashen when they told her that Doctor Brown had died in the gunfight. The courier Eilene Hamstead was shaken too, but more, Forster assumed, by the abrupt arrival of the police, and all the subsequent violence, than she was by Brown's death; as a newcomer to the Oberhauser environment, presumably with no reason to suspect that the police had managed to piece together some of what was going on, it had to have been a stunning revelation when Forster and Blaine pushed their way inside the house with arrest warrants.

Nor could it have helped much that neither of the detectives said a word for the full distance back to Wilshire Division. Forster, who had killed a man, did not feel talkative, and John Blaine, who was not as concerned over the killing as he was anxious over Kramer's escape, was also preoccupied.

Even when they took the pair of women along to be booked, and afterwards called for a matron to come up to the office and be present during the interrogation, neither detective said much.

Both women seemed as unnerved by the

grave faces and the drawn-out silences, as they did by their earlier experience of being inside the house while that furious and deadly gun battle had been in progress outside.

Forster also called Ben Hastings's office, so that he could sit in on this interrogation if he chose to, but Hastings was out of the building, Virginia said, and probably would do no more than check in about quitting time, before heading for home.

Forster asked Virginia to contact the steno pool and have a girl come up who was authorized to notarize signatures, then he rang off.

John went next door and returned with four cups of coffee, which he distributed. The plain-looking pseudo maid smiled coolly in appreciation, but Irene Oberhauser hardly more than glanced round as she accepted the cup. Her attention was fully upon Reg Forster, as it had been on her earlier visit to the office.

She finally said, 'We knew absolutely nothing about what was going to happen, Inspector Forster. Nothing at all.'

Reg studied the flawless features in silence, for a moment, before holding out his hand to John. Blaine fished the ruby ring from a pocket, dropped it upon his partner's palm, and Forster, watcning Irene Oberhauser's face, placed a fingerpad upon the red stone, and pressed. The stone, held upright in the setting by a tiny steel spring, yielded and sank down inside the setting. Forster then put the ring upon his desktop in plain sight.

'When they've stripped Brown at the coroner's office, Mrs Oberhauser, we'll have everything he was wearing put through the police laboratory. Did you know that the Los Angeles Police Department has one of the finest forensic and criminal labs in the country? Doctor Brown's wristwatch will be put through—along with this ring.'

The beautiful woman said, 'I've already told Inspector Blaine the ring was electronically capable of signalling Doctor Brown, through his watch. But all that proves is that, the way crime now is in the city, people have to resort to these measures to protect themselves— because, obviously, the police can't do the job. Or *won't* do the job.'

Reg and John Blaine turned as the police matron and the stenographer appeared in the doorway. Both women glanced at the prisoners, said nothing to either of them, and took chairs as though they were going through a routine completely commonplace to them both. Irene and the pseudo maid watched the stenographer open her book and sit, pencil poised. Only when Forster spoke again, did the women look back at him.

He told the prisoners they could make this interview short or long. 'It's up to you. You are also entitled to have counsel present, although this is not an official interrogation.'

Mrs Oberhauser arched an eyebrow. 'What is it, then?' she asked.

Forster's answer was short. 'All you have to do is listen.' He glanced at the typewritten page in front of him atop the desk, and said, 'The woman Eilene Hamstead arrived in Los Angeles day before yesterday, by air, filed an application for domestic work the same day with an employment agency, giving her preference as the Westwood area. You called in to hire a maid to replace Peggy Bryan, picked up Miss Hamstead today, and she drove home with you. Meanwhile, Peggy Bryan, dressed as a man by Doctor Brown, was put aboard an aircraft for New York City—with a message in code inside the locking mechanism of her flight bag.'

Forster paused to raise his eyes to the beautiful woman. She was watching him intently, her face still pale, but otherwise stone-set and impassive. Forster went on speaking, then.

'Harold Oberhauser, driving a car taken from the motor pool at Oberhauser Industries, was picked up by a seaplane between Ventura and Santa Barbara, and the man at the morgue was a former Polish seaman ... As for the Organization, we're going to contact the FBI and the New York authorities with what we now know about it, and they can go from there.' He looked from Irene Oberhauser to the plain-looking girl, and got a surprise.

Eilene Hamstead, speaking in a hard voice, said, 'You do whatever you want to do, but I'll tell you one thing, the Organization can't be broken. Maybe you and the other Establishment gestapo agencies can hurt us a little, but we'll go underground, and keep right on working for the liberation of the people!'

John Blaine listened, studied the girl for a moment, then dug out a cigar and lit up, rolling his eyes round to Reg, who swung his chair half around almost without thinking about it, and shoved the window open. Forster studied Eilene thoughtfully, and arrived at a conclusion: *This* one was not going to yield; no matter what Irene did, and no matter what Peggy Bryan or any of the others might do, *this* member of the Organization was not going to co-operate.

Fortunately, she was not very high in the Organization's hierarchy. He returned his attention to Irene Oberhauser, and for the balance of the interview, almost completely ignored the Hamstead woman.

'Where is Kramer?' he asked, and got a shrug of indifference and no answer. He nodded at Blaine, 'Call downstairs for an All Points Bulletin on both Kramer and Oberhauser. You may as well alert all airport facilities about the seaplane too, John. Maybe the Air Force's coastal defence units can make a search.'

Blaine picked up his telephone as Forster

129

slowly shook his head at the beautiful woman. 'You're on the losing side. You are implicated up to your neck in what Harold Oberhauser has been doing. You are directly implicated in the death of Henry Brown—also known as Heinrich Braun—and his attack upon police officers. You could help yourself, and us, at the same time, by explaining one thing: why did Brown come on like a gangbuster; why did he attempt to shoot it out with us?'

Eilene Hamstead interrupted. 'You don't have to answer that question,' she told the older woman. 'You don't have to answer any questions at all. They're violating our rights by using gestapo interrogation methods without allowing us counsel.'

Forster ignored the Hamstead woman and did not take his eyes off Irene Oberhauser as he said, 'As I said, this isn't an interrogation. I want you to know what the police have against you, Mrs Oberhauser, and tonight, when you're locked in, you can think it over. Maybe, by morning, you'll see things differently.' Forster watched the handsome face, the steady, large eyes. He was gambling on the fact that, to a woman as handsome, and as inevitably egotistical, as this former dancer had to be, the dark-night, jail-cell thoughts of long imprisonment would prove overwhelmingly horrible. Irene Oberhauser, like most beautiful women, had to be too self-centred, too convinced of her personal value, to be able to see herself as a martyr. He did not believe she could ever accept the thought of self-sacrifice. But it was a gamble; he had been wrong in his judgements of people before. He might be wrong again.

'As for the Organization,' he told her. 'Someone's mistake put your head in the lion's mouth.'

'What mistake?' challenged the Hamstead woman.

Forster answered without looking away from Irene Oberhauser. 'The murdered man's plastic surgery was very good, but plastic surgery is detectable, Mrs Oberhauser. That wasn't what fouled you up, though. Fingerprints can't be changed. It's been tried a dozen different ways, from using acid, to paraffin tips. In this case, though, the negligence was either plain stupid, or deliberately stupid; anyone ought to realize that a murder victim is put through every kind of a police examination. *Looking* like someone else, isn't enough.'

The telephone rang and Forster leaned to lift it, still without taking his eyes off the handsome former dancer. Ben Hastings was now in his office, and was calling to be brought up to date. When Forster told him what had happened at the Oberhauser residence, Hastings asked what was being done to locate Kramer. When Forster explained, Captain

Hastings said, 'We can't take a chance on losing another one, Reg. I'll call in the CIA.' Then Hastings rang off, precluding any argument, and Forster put down his telephone with John gazing at him quizzically. Reg said, 'You'd better go up the hall.' Blaine nodded and arose to depart.

Both women were watching Forster closely now. They had heard one side of the telephone conversation, which had to be tantalizing to them, and now Forster leaned back in his chair, gazing steadily at Irene Oberhauser through a long moment of silence, while he arrived at the conclusion that he had said just about all he could say in his effort to shake her, except for one more thing, so he threw that in, too, before turning the prisoners over to the matron.

'I think you had better hope the police find your husband before the other people do, Mrs Oberhauser.'

Then Forster sat forward and arose to stand behind the desk. The reaction to this last statement got a reaction, not from Irene Oberhauser, but from the hostile pseudo maid, Eilene Hamstead. She blurted out a hostile and defiant statement. 'They'll never find him. Never!'

The Hamstead woman arose, glaring her defiance. Forster shrugged and nodded to the matron. He leaned to pick up the Bryan woman's statement as all four of the women

132

turned to leave the office. He only looked up when Irene Oberhauser seemed to pause in the doorway. They exchanged a look, then Irene, prodded by the matron, departed, and the last woman to leave, the stenographer, closed the door after herself.

Forster gave them a couple of minutes, then he too left the office. He went up to the far end of the corridor, winked at Captain Hastings's receptionist, and knocked once before opening the captain's door and entering.

Ben and John Blaine watched Forster stride over where an empty chair stood near the window, and sit down, as he said, 'I have a feeling we might be able to crack the Oberhauser woman, but that other one—unless she wanted to talk, I doubt that wild horses could drag a statement out of her.'

The telephone rang on Hastings's desk. He picked it up, said his name, listened, then slowly swivelled his gaze around and held out the telephone towards Forster.

'Downstairs,' the captain said. 'The matron who just turned your prisoners over to the jailer.'

Forster took the telephone and gave his name. A woman's hard, flat-toned voice said, 'Inspector, the Oberhauser woman asked for some Valium. Down here, where we handle them like carloads of beef, that usually means a very bad case of nerves. I just thought I'd let you know.'

Forster had a sudden thought. 'Can you get her to the telephone?' he asked.

The matron said, 'Yes; hang on a moment.'

It was more than a moment, but eventually Irene Oberhauser's strained, thin-sounding voice came up to Forster. He said, 'Mrs Oberhauser, there is one thing I neglected to tell you in my office. If the police hang back a little, I'm sure your husband is going to be run down by the people who are after him . . . The *Arcana* people.' He put down the telephone without allowing the woman to say a word, then, under the puzzled looks of Hastings and Blaine, he started back towards the chair. But he did not quite reach it before the telephone rang again. This time, as Captain Hastings put the instrument to his ear, he did not get the chance fully to pronounce his name before a female voice, running her words all together, called for Inspector Forster. Hastings held out the phone again.

Forster went back, spoke his name, and Irene Oberhauser said, 'That was a threat, Inspector. That was blackmail, when you said if the police hung back a little. You *want* the Arcana people to find my husband; you *want* him killed.'

Forster, ignoring the stares of Hastings and Blaine, answered quietly. 'No such a thing. But they know more about him than we do. All we know is that this entire thing was engineered to throw them off his track. Mrs Oberhauser, we can't prevent the newspapers from publishing the story about the man at the coroner's office whose fingerprints do not match the prints of Harold Oberhauser. A story like that is far too bizarre to be passed up by the wire services. It'll make the New York newspapers in a day or two. *Then* the people who know all about Harold Oberhauser, will be after him all over again, and we'll have to hang back, because we just do not know as much about him as they do.'

'. . . Inspector, can you have me brought to your office without Eilene Hamstead knowing about it?'

Forster turned an ironic look upon John Blaine. 'Yes, Mrs Oberhauser, it can be arranged.'

'Then please do it, right away.'

Forster put down the telephone, and, speaking quietly, told the other two men what had just happened. Captain Hastings did not look as pleased as Blaine did. Hastings garrulously said, 'Fine. You're coming out of this rather well, Reg. Except for one thing. Except for two things: Oberhauser and Kramer.' He arose. 'I'll go sit in on the meeting with you. John, ask Virginia to call down and arrange for a matron and a steno to be sent up to your office, will you?'

CHAPTER FIFTEEN

THE BREAKTHROUGH

The first thing Irene Oberhauser told Reg
Forster, in front of a matron, a police
stenographer, Captain Hastings and John
Blaine, took a great load off Forster's mind.
She said that Joseph Kramer had left the
Oberhauser residence at least two hours
before the police arrived. Which meant, of
course, that Kramer could not know, yet, that
Henry Brown had been killed resisting the
police, or that Irene, and Eilene Hamstead,
were in police custody.

The next thing she said made Forster forget
his mild elation. 'You asked why Henry Brown
used a gun when the police arrived . . . He told
me about a half hour earlier to pack and be
ready to leave when he came round in his car.
He did not tell me the whole story, but the
message Eilene Hamstead brought with her
was a firm warning that someone out here on
the West Coast had sold us out to Arcana, and
when Henry came over to tell me that, and to
make plans for our flight, he could not find
Joseph anywhere. He got very upset. He said it
must have been Joseph who had sold us out.
He ran back to get his car. Eilene and I were
in the back of the house packing when you and

136

Inspector Blaine arrived, and entered the house ... When those other two detectives, whom Henry did not know, came skulking into the garden, I'm sure he thought they were Arcana's assassins. That's why he tried to shoot them ... To gain enough time for the three of us to escape.'

Forster felt Ben Hastings's eyes on his face, but ignored this to ask Irene Oberhauser a question. 'Do you believe Kramer sold your husband out?'

Irene shook her head. 'Never. Not for one moment, and that's what I told Henry, but he was past being reasoned with. Inspector, Joseph was as loyal to my husband as it was possible for a man to be ... Inspector ... ?'

'Yes.'

The steady, large eyes wavered for the first time, when Forster and Irene Oberhauser were together. Then she resumed speaking, but in a lower tone of voice. 'It was Joseph who killed the man sent on from New York to impersonate my husband. He told Harold that it was the only way to throw the Arcana people completely off Harold's trail.'

Hastings had a question. 'Did the Organization know this impersonator was to be killed?'

Irene shook her head. 'No.' She looked back at Forster again. 'He was supposed to take Harold's place, and make it appear that he was fleeing, so the Arcana people would pursue him. That was all. Harold spoke to some of the directors back in New York. This was their scheme, and while the impersonator was leading the assassins away, Harold was to fly back to New York where the Organization could put him out of sight for a year or two ... The killing was spontaneous. Well, *almost* spontaneous. Joseph, Henry, Harold and I, had a meeting. Joseph said that even if the impersonator managed to lead the assassins on a wild goose chase, it still would not take Harold's name off the Arcana list of victims. He said he had a better plan ... *Harold*, not the impersonator, would flee, and Joseph would kill the impersonator, which would convince Arcana that Harold was dead ... I don't know why someone didn't think about the different fingerprints, Inspector. Probably because we were all so upset. Harold and Henry Brown had been years building up their cover, Henry as a very respectable physicist and college instructor, and Harold as a prominent industrialist.'

Hastings had another question. 'If Brown knew all this, why would he imagine Kramer had sold you out?'

Irene Oberhauser had no answer. 'I don't know. Too many things happened, too fast. I don't know why some of them happened. I'm sorry ...'

Forster spoke up. 'Arcana. What, exactly, is it, Mrs Oberhauser?'

She seemed momentarily to look through and beyond Forster before speaking again, and Forster got the feeling that, whatever Arcana was, Irene Oberhauser feared it very much.

'It's an underground organization; people who survived the German concentration camps head it up. They seem to be just about everywhere. In Europe, in the United States, in South and Central America ... In the Middle East. Harold told me once that he thought most of the financing came from the Middle East.'

'A large organization,' murmured John Blaine, and Irene Oberhauser shot him a look, shaking her head.

'No, that's what makes it almost impossible for the Organization to create defences; it's not large, but it is wealthy. For twenty-five years its organizers have been hunting down former German concentration camp personnel. Like my husband.'

Forster said, 'To assassinate them?'

'Yes. Henry Brown had a list that he showed Harold about a year ago. My husband was not a fearful man, but for a few days after he saw that list, he was actually afraid. He told me he'd seen names on Henry's list of people he had known, had worked with at Neuengamme.'

'This list,' stated Ben Hastings, 'was of names of people Arcana had had killed?'

'Yes,' replied the beautiful woman. 'It was

given to Henry on one of his visits to the east coast, by one of the Organization's executives.'

'The Organization,' said Hastings, 'being a communist infiltration consortium of some kind; right?'

Irene watched John Blaine drain his coffee cup before gently inclining her head. She began speaking again after what seemed to Reg Forster to be an interlude of rallying. 'My husband, and the others, were recruited into the Soviet espionage service during the last months of the war ... It was not a difficult choice for them. I've heard Harold and Henry Brown say that their real enemy had always been the United States; that if the United States had not allied itself with Britain, and also with the Soviet Union, Germany could have won. They hated the United States.'

Forster and Hastings exchanged a glance. Hastings said, 'Mrs Oberhauser; what are *your* feelings about this?'

Forster thought he knew what her answer would be, and he was correct. She said, 'I—a wife's first loyalty is to her husband. I—didn't *like* some of Harold's ideas, but he was always so rational, so well-informed and so wise. He said that he had been on the losing side once, and he would never be on that side again. He told me the Soviet Union *had* to win, because the Americans did not have the stomach nor the endurance to wage either a long, drawn-out secret war, or a prolonged fighting war ...

I didn't argue ... I didn't agree, but I didn't argue. Then, when the Korean War and the Vietnamese War came along ... I knew my husband was right.' Irene raised her head and stared steadily at Reg Forster, in that peculiarly intent way she had of regarding him.

For a moment she was silent, then she suddenly said, 'You knew about the seaplane. Did you know the rest of it; that my husband was to be taken north along the coast of Canada, and put aboard a Soviet fishing trawler?'

Forster had not known this, of course, or he would have tried to prevent it, but not actually because he wanted to get custody of Harold Oberhauser for being an enemy agent, but because it seemed that the only person who could give direct testimony against the murderer, Joseph Kramer, was his fellow-conspirator in the killing, Harold Oberhauser.

Ben Hastings arose and without a word, left the room. Blaine and Forster exchanged a look, they could guess what Hastings was going to do. Forster had a private hunch Hastings would not succeed; Oberhauser had far too much of a head-start.

John Blaine asked a question of Irene Oberhauser. The same question Reg Forster would have asked, if John hadn't. 'Where did Kramer go?'

'I think Henry Brown could have told you that,' the woman replied, 'but he's dead. I don't know. I suspect that Joseph began to think the whole West Coast unit was doomed the moment my husband slipped away. You should remember that Joseph survived something very few German soldiers managed to live through, captivity in the Soviet Union immediately after the German defeat in Russia. Joseph had a terribly strong instinct for survival. Harold told me that several times. Personally, I believe Joseph probably went after my husband. I suspected he might do something like that. In fact, I mentioned it to Henry, but he scoffed at the idea.'

John Blaine yawned, glanced at his wrist, glanced at the shadows beyond the back-wall window, and until he did those things, Forster had not been the least bit aware of the time.

He wanted to hear more, but for the time being he knew enough. He said, 'We'll have this conversation worked up into a deposition, Mrs Oberhauser, and submit it to you for your consideration.' He smiled and stood up. 'Tomorrow we'll see about going through it all again, in the presence of an attorney.'

The beautiful, statuesque woman stood up. 'I don't want an attorney,' she said to Forster. 'I want to co-operate . . . I don't want to go to prison and rot there.'

Reg shrugged, caught the matron's eye and nodded. He waited until the women had gone, then he said, 'Maybe she doesn't *want* a lawyer but she's damned well going to *get* one. John, this is one case we're not going to have thrown out of court because some lawyer insists his client's rights were violated.'

Blaine arose. 'You got any idea what time it is?'

Forster started to raise his arm to look at his wrist, when Ben Hastings pushed into the office from the corridor with a crisp statement. 'The Oberhauser woman was correct. I checked with the Coast Guard and they've had a Soviet trawler under surveillance most of the day, then, late this afternoon when it made a sudden run towards our coast up north, along a lonely long stretch of uninhabited shoreline, the Guard sent in one of its ships, and the trawler turned and made a fast run out to sea.' Captain Hastings offered a pithy smile. 'The Coast Guard seamen spotted an aircraft heading low over the water for the trawler, but when they appeared, and the Russians turned-tail, the aircraft made a big turn and headed back inland again. The Coast Guard radioed for help from the Civil Aeronautics Authority.'

Blaine, who was hanging on every word, now said, 'Did they get him?'

Hastings nodded slowly. 'They let the trawler get away, but they nailed the seaplane. It couldn't land just anywhere. They trailed it to a lake north-east of San Francisco, put down beside it, placed the pilot and his passenger under arrest, and—'

143

'Oberhauser?' blurted out John Blaine.

Hastings nodded. 'Yeah. They're bringing him over here . . . John, it's past quitting time.'

Blaine, who had indirectly complained about this long day only a short while earlier, now shook his head as though he had never had any such thoughts. 'I'll just call my wife,' he said, leaning for the telephone. Over his bent form Hastings and Reg Forster exchanged amused smiles.

Outside, the spent day had departed, the city was aglow with lights and, as Forster stood by the window gazing out, he remembered the captain's earlier appeal to the CIA for immediate help, and turned to ask about that.

Ben Hastings, in the act of lighting a cigar, looked up. 'I didn't call them. I was *going* to. I *meant* to.' He finished lighting up, and examined the evenly glowing end of his cigar. 'They'll have a man around here first thing in the morning.' His eyes came up. 'We're entitled to do *our* thing, too, aren't we?'

Forster grinned, and returned to his desk without commenting.

CHAPTER SIXTEEN

A MATTER OF CO-OPERATION

Wilshire Division's second floor Homicide Division was not the first agency to monitor the Coast Guard's interception, in fact it was the *last* agency to accomplish this. The first outside bureau to be notified of any Coast Guard activity against foreign shipping was the Central Intelligence Agency and no sooner had Ben Hastings made his contact with the Guard's local office, than the CIA resident spook in Los Angeles, called Hastings, and was put through to the office of Forster and Blaine.

It was CIA policy, when approaching other law enforcement bureaux, to identify itself as an off-shoot of NSA, the National Security Agency, which as a matter of fact it was, and to leave little doubt in anyone's mind that any matters considered irregular in relation to US laws or national safety, were strictly CIA responsibilities.

All this was explained to Captain Hastings as though he were totally ignorant of it, by the CIA representative who called. Almost any other time of the day, or the evening, Captain Hastings might have duly acknowledged it without rancour, but the voice at the other end of the connection sounded too young, the tone of voice was too patronizing, and the re-stating of ancient fact, was a little too offensive. So, with Forster and Blaine listening, Hastings said, 'Listen, sonny, any time there's been a murder in my territory, my department gets involved. As for the cloak-and-dagger stuff, you're welcome to it; one of your spooks is due round here in the morning. We'll certainly co-operate—but tonight we're working on a local homicide, and regardless, we're going to keep right on working on it.'

Hastings put down the telephone, plugged the cigar back into his mouth, looked a trifle sulphurously at the other two men in the small office, then sighed and said, 'That's the trouble with being good-natured, people tend to walk over you.'

No one disputed this statement; the 'good-natured' bureau chief just did not look like a man to be disputed with right at the moment. Then, having disposed of this interruption, he said, 'Oberhauser ought to be an interesting conversationalist. I wouldn't miss this if I had to sit up all night.'

Blaine said, 'You probably will have to, Captain,' and Reg Forster captured their attention by speaking of something altogether different.

'I would like very much to know what's become of Joseph Kramer. Obviously he wasn't on the seaplane with Oberhauser.'

146

Blaine had a suggestion. 'He's running like a scairt rabbit.'

Forster gazed dispassionately at his associate officer. 'Give the devil his due, John. No one runs scared who fought through all the battles up to the gates of Moscow.'

Ben Hastings seemed to agree, as he sat, smoking and gazing beyond Forster into the darkness beyond the window.

The telephone rang, Forster hoisted it, listened a moment, put the telephone down and arose from behind his desk. 'That was fast,' he told the other two men. 'They brought Oberhauser down by air.'

Hastings straightened up. 'Where is he?'

'Downstairs, being booked in,' said Forster. They all three headed for the door at the same time, Captain Hastings leaving his cigar in the glass ashtray atop John Blaine's desk.

Not until they were trotting down the stairs did Hastings mention the kind of thing which would occur to a police department chief. 'If they grabbed him up north somewhere, and whisked him down here, a lawyer could make something out of that; extradition under duress, maybe?'

Forster made no comment, neither did John Blaine. There were any number of times during the course of almost any homicide assignment when the niceties of the law made every investigator's blood boil, and that went without saying.

147

When they got down there, Forster's first view of Harold Oberhauser was startling, because Oberhauser was an exact duplicate of the man on the coroner's slab. It was a little like witnessing a resurrection. However, *this* Harold Oberhauser was haggard; he looked like a man who had survived too many crises in too short a period of time. He was in the custody of a beefy FBI agent, who introduced himself as Carl Eddington. He and Captain Hastings walked off a short distance so as not to be overheard, and conversed for a short while. Forster and Blaine strolled over where a booking sergeant was shoving papers at Oberhauser to be signed. As the detectives walked up, Oberhauser glanced round at them and calmly said, 'I suppose now that it is all over, eh?' He did not appear to want, or expect, an answer, and turned back to signing the papers.

Forster and the booking sergeant exchanged a look and Forster nodded in a way the sergeant appeared to understand, even before Forster said, 'If you have no objection, Ed, we'll take him upstairs for a while.'

The sergeant shrugged. 'Take your time.'

Forster smiled. 'You'll get him back for the full treatment a little later.' The sergeant was already placing the papers pertaining to Oberhauser to one side, atop his desk, with the air of a man to whom this kind of irregularity was not, really, all that irregular, where

Homicide Division was concerned.

The FBI agent departed. Captain Hastings strolled over, studied Oberhauser in silence, then introduced himself, without the customary handshake, and preceded them all back up the stairs and down the lighted corridor. Only once did Harold Oberhauser speak. That was when they reached the landing and he was shoulder-to-shoulder with Reg Forster. He looked around and said, 'Where is my wife?'

To answer that question posed no problem; not the way it would have, if he'd asked about Henry Brown. Reg said, 'Downstairs, locked up.'

Oberhauser gazed a moment longer at Forster, then stoically followed Ben Hastings to the nearby office, and when Ben pointed to a chair, Oberhauser sat down with the look of a man who was relieved that now, at long last, he could stop moving, could stop getting up and sitting down, stop running.

Ben Hastings, wise in the way of his vocation, passed the initiative to Reg Forster with only a look. Forster faced Oberhauser near his desk, leaning, over there.

'Your wife, the latest courier from New York, Eilene Hamstead—if that's her name—plus your former maid, Peggy Bryan, are all in cells downstairs, Mr Oberhauser ... and Henry Brown is dead, killed in a fight with the police in your rear garden today.'

The last bit of information seemed temporarily to stun Oberhauser. He continued to stare at Forster for almost a half minute after Reg had stopped speaking to step behind his desk, sit down back there, and fish through his top desk drawer for the Intelligence report on Oberhauser.

Then the dishevelled man dully said, 'I was right, wasn't I? It *is* all over.'

Forster did not answer. He flicked through the report and spoke without raising his eyes. 'The government is interested in you, and I rather imagine they'll be round in the morning to pick you up.' Reg raised his head a little. 'Where is Joseph Kramer?'

All three of the detectives saw Oberhauser's eyes widen perceptibly. 'Where . . . ? If you have the others, then you must also have Kramer,' stated the industrialist.

'He left not long after you did, Mr Oberhauser. It's possible that he saw the handwriting on the wall before the rest of you did. At least he certainly didn't waste any time in disappearing.'

Oberhauser's retort was short and believable. 'I have no idea . . . Do you have statements?'

'Yes. From Peggy Bryan and also from your wife. Your wife filled us in as to details. She also told us of the meeting you had with the others, when Kramer advanced the suggestion of killing the Polish seaman who was to

150

impersonate you.'

Oberhauser said, 'I see,' in a tired-sounding voice. 'Did she tell you who actually shot the Pole?'

'Kramer,' replied Forster, and leaned on the desk watching the older man. 'One thing she hasn't told us yet, and she may not even know it, but I'm sure you can clear it up. What, exactly, was Kramer's position with the Organization, out here on the West Coast?'

Oberhauser's mouth drooped when he uttered one word. 'Assassin.'

Forster glanced at Hastings. The captain nodded, but took no part in the conversation at this point.

Blaine had a question. 'You knew Kramer better than anyone; where would he go, if he was running?'

Oberhauser gently shook his head. 'I don't know.'

'We think he might have tried to connect up with you,' stated Blaine, and Oberhauser turned a slow gaze in John's direction.

'How? He didn't know where I was going.'

Blaine was not convinced of this. '*Someone* knew, Mr Oberhauser, otherwise you couldn't have co-ordinated the seaplane-pickup so well, with the arrival of the Soviet trawler. If a couple of people know things, it's usually fairly safe to assume others will also know. How did you notify the people in New York to get you out by seaplane?'

'Very simply,' replied Oberhauser. 'I picked up the telephone and called them. It was an inexcusable breach of training and Organization policy, but things were moving to a head too fast for the regular channels.' Oberhauser shrugged. 'I didn't even know they would be able to help, but I called in, told them my course of flight, then I took a company car and ran for it ... And I almost made it.' Oberhauser turned back to Forster. 'Joseph is a master of survival, you know.'

Forster had never for one moment doubted this, but he knew with an equal conviction, that the day of the fleeing fugitive was long past. Electronics, plus a vast and complicated—and highly efficient—police network, nationwide, made continued flight impossible. He also knew, from experience with organized crime, that every illegal syndicate had contingency plans, and he suspected that this obtained perhaps even more with the kind of illegal organization he was now dealing with, so he said, 'Mr Oberhauser, Joseph Kramer is a disciplined man. He didn't just jump into a car and go racing off, blindly.'

'Inspector,' said the older man, completely recovered now from the shock of those earlier revelations concerning the disintegration of his West Coast cell, 'you said it, yourself—he was probably trying to connect up with me.'

Forster did not argue this point. 'If I had *all* the answers, we wouldn't be sitting here now, would we?' Reg smiled. 'If we don't find him, Arcana will.'

Oberhauser rebutted that almost wearily. 'His name is not on their list.' Then he rallied, and said, 'And you can't prove he shot the impersonator, either.'

Reg continued to smile. 'We're not spy-catchers, we're homicide investigators. On the subversion and espionage angles, we can be faulted, but not on the angles having to do with murder. Mr Oberhauser, you have a choice; help us find him, or along with the other charges they'll levy against you, will be a charge of complicity in murder, and obstructing justice.'

Oberhauser looked bewildered. 'If I'm not already under arrest for complicity, what *am* I charged with?'

Captain Hastings answered that. 'You're being held on two warrants, one originated with us, the other one was given me downstairs by the FBI agent who brought you down here. It's for illegal flight to avoid prosecution as a foreign agent. In the morning there will be another one, no doubt; a hold-order by the Central Intelligence Agency.' Hastings paused a moment, then said, 'The CIA doesn't prosecute through courts of law. They hand all their evidence over to the FBI, who do the prosecuting. Take my word for it, Mr Oberhauser, if the CIA wants you, they'll work up one hell of a case for the prosecution.

153

Would you care for some unsolicited advice?'

Oberhauser said, 'What is it?'

Hastings said, 'Co-operate. Any way you look at it, you've lost. By now the CIA, in conjunction with the FBI, will be rounding up Organization people on the East Coast. Tomorrow, they'll fan out, here on the West Coast. By tomorrow night your outfit will be busted down to the man who answers the door and empties the ashtrays.' Captain Hastings brought forth a cigar from an inside jacket pocket and held it in his hands as he said, 'Under the law, Mr Oberhauser, you're entitled to a lawyer, which I'm sure you understand, and you're also eligible for bail, which means you will be freed, probably tomorrow, pending your preliminary court hearing.' Hastings took his time lighting the cigar before saying anything more, then, as the smoke arose, he made his point. 'You can co-operate, and be held here in a maximum security cell—or you'll be turned out of here tomorrow—and the newspapers will carry the whole damned story about you having been impersonated, and being still alive . . . How many of Arcana's assassins do you suppose are here, in the city, reading our daily newspapers?'

Harold Oberhauser looked steadily at Captain Hastings through an interlude of long silence, then he slowly inclined his head.

'I'll co-operate,' he said.

CHAPTER SEVENTEEN

THE MANHUNT!

It was late, and getting later by the moment. In any case, Harold Oberhauser was worn down, not by anything the police had done, but by a series of psychological body-blows over the past twenty-four hours, which had to have been stunning to him. All his years of carefully creating a very sophisticated cover, all his years of feeling entirely safe, all his successes as the agent of a foreign nation, had come to an abrupt end, and, ironically, it was nothing he had done within the past quarter century which had caused this sequence of disasters, it was something he had done *before*, something he had been a part of so long ago that most of the people he met from day to day, only knew of such things through history books. If Harold Oberhauser had ever questioned the Law of Retribution, he certainly knew now that there was such a law, and that regardless of how long it took for it to manifest, ultimately, it *did* work. Like an echo from the distant past, all those deaths he had known of at Neuengamme, all those people he had seen go to the cremation ovens, all those wretched sufferers who had perished from over-work, starvation, and brutality, were now exacting

155

payment. Death was the echo.

He was a tired man; he had aged very much over the past week, but particularly over the past twenty-four hours. He must have realized that the sooner all this was concluded, the sooner another unpleasant phase of his existence would end. Like a man hoping for salvation, he brought the interlude in Forster's office to a close with a simple statement.

'As you've said, Inspector Forster, there was a contingency plan. I don't know that Joseph used it. I really meant it when I told you I have no idea where he went. But, in the event of a real disaster, we were all to escape as best we could, and rendezvous up the coast, inland five or six miles from a place called Sycamore Canyon. There is a ridge of bare stone up there from which it is possible to see in all directions for hundreds of miles, but mainly, the ridge commands an unobstructed view of a length of ocean-front beach which is both uninhabited, and has a number of deepwater inlets. There is a cabin below the ridge in a hidden fold in the hills. In fact, I've flown over it, and the cabin isn't visible from the air.'

Captain Hastings said, 'Radio equipment up there, Mr Oberhauser?' and when the German nodded, Ben glanced at Forster, 'And of course, there would be trawlers off-shore somewhere, especially now, if Kramer's up there sending out a May-Day call for help.' Hastings glanced at his wrist, sighed, arose from the chair and said, 'John; take Mr Oberhauser back down to booking, will you, then meet us out back at the car.' Hastings stepped to Forster's desk and reached for the telephone as Blaine and Harold Oberhauser headed for the door. Hastings called the sheriff's department, which had jurisdiction in the county, outside the city limits, and asked for the name and extension-number of the officer in charge of the coastal area north of Santa Monica to the Ventura County boundary line. It required ten minutes for Captain Hastings to locate the right man, and explain the situation, and by that time Blaine had got rid of his companion in booking, and was ambling out back.

He was standing there, in the warm, moonless night, hands in trouser pockets, looking pensive, when Hastings and Forster arrived. Without a word, Hastings slid behind the wheel, the other two detectives climbed in, and they drove out of the parking area.

Traffic was light, for a change, probably because of the lateness of the hour. They made excellent time, once they got upon the carriageway leading from Wilshire Division in the direction of Westwood, and beyond, down to the coast highway through slumbering Santa Monica, another of those former drowsy enclaves which had been quietly swallowed by burgeoning, greater Los Angeles, until its former pleasant individuality had been layered over with the anonymity of the immense slum-sprawl which was the City of Los Angeles.

They were boring through the salt-scented ocean air northward, when Blaine leaned upon the back of the front seat to ask if Captain Hastings knew where this place was, Oberhauser had mentioned. The captain's reply was matter-of-fact.

'Yeah. Believe it or not, John, when you were still hoeing corn-rows back in Indiana, I was hunting rabbits in the Malibu hills.'

Blaine continued to lean while he ran this through his mind, until he finally said, 'I'm from Ohio, not Indiana, and I never hoed any corn in my life. I was born and raised in the city.' Then, having cleared this up, he also said, 'I didn't know you were a native Californian.' He sounded so surprised that Ben Hastings shot him a look in the rearview mirror, but said nothing more. But it was true; ninety-nine residents of California out of a hundred had been born elsewhere; natives were still scarce enough to be an oddity, at least in *Southern* California.

Reg Forster, only an indifferent listener to this short exchange, said, 'And suppose Kramer's not up here?'

Hastings had an answer for that. 'Then one of us will stay with their short-wave set, until the CIA can get up here. Maybe the government will want to play games with the trawlers. In World War Two, in Europe, they called it *Funkspiel.'* Hastings raised his eyes to the rearview mirror again. 'John; you didn't know I was in ETO during the war, did you?'

Blaine, looking blank, said, 'ETO?'

'European Theatre of Operations.' Hastings made a loud groan. 'I keep forgetting, you're too young to remember. I was a communications sergeant in ETO for the Allies; we tried to capture kraut communications systems and feed back a lot of misinformation. The krauts called it *Funkspiel.'*

Blaine said, *'Funkspiel.* That's sure a crummy language, isn't it. *Funkspiel*; sounds like something I caught once, off a toilet seat, and had to take antibiotic shots for three months to cure.'

Hastings glanced at the man beside him on the front seat. Forster glanced back, amused, then Hastings put all his attention upon driving.

The distance from Wilshire Division to the canyon Oberhauser had identified was considerable, but once they had cleared Santa Monica, and were heading north up the Coast Highway, the miles slipped rearward quite rapidly. It was only about thirty miles or so from Santa Monica to the Ventura County line, and Sycamore Canyon was roughly a mile south of the line.

It also happened to be one of those turn-offs that, unless a person were watching closely, even in broad daylight, or knew precisely where it was, could slip past unnoticed.

Ben Hastings, though, proved his knowledgeability by slackening speed a mile before they reached the dark, narrow opening, where an oiled road went twisting and turning inland from some cliffs overlooking the Pacific Ocean, which was on their left as they reached the canyon, and turned up it.

Almost immediately, they had the ocean behind them, lost beyond the maze of brushy hills. There was a meagre watercourse in the bottom of the canyon on their left, as they climbed steadily, and scattered at random over its full length were unkempt-looking, tall old sycamore trees. Forster, able to see only the nearest trees as they wound their way uphill, surmised that this was where the canyon had probably got its name, but he was wrong. Sycamore Canyon's *real* name was Yerba Buena, but the highway road-signs, as well as the few, spotty residents of this coast range of mountains, used the newer name.

There were only two or three sets of buildings visible from the road for the first few miles, and by the time the ocean was lost in the background, beyond the high, rolling swells of land, Forster had forgotten all about its proximity, until Hastings, pointing to a raw, rugged upthrust of pure rock on their left, said, 'Boney Ridge. That's the rim Oberhauser meant when he said you could see in all directions from up here. Mainly, you can see the ocean for several hundred miles, on a clear day.'

Blaine, leaning to peer from the window on his left, made a practical suggestion. 'Okay. Now we know what ridge he meant. Just where the hell is this cabin, or whatever it is, where Kramer's supposed to be—or do we climb that lousy mountain and look down into some canyon to find it?'

Hastings's answer was brusque. 'There aren't more than three or four cabins on the far side of that ridge. We just pick the right one.'

'How?' demanded John.

Hastings smiled crookedly. 'By eliminating the first three. Two of them are lived in, or were the last time I was up here. There's another one, not lived in, a fellow built years ago out of log slabs. He ran cattle through these mountains.'

'That's the one, then?' Blaine said.

'Nope,' Hastings answered, without explaining why this wouldn't be their goal. 'The place where Kramer *ought* to be, is up a very old trail, around a sidehill, and down where there's a spring coming out of the rocks.'

Blaine frowned. 'Why not the one made of slabs, then?'

'No water,' stated Captain Hastings. 'John, you've got to have water, and through these

161

hills there's precious damned little of it.'

They left the car where the road turned abruptly, up near the canyon's topmost rims, and, with Ben Hastings in the lead, struck out over a dusty trail with flourishing underbrush growing on both sides of it, manhigh in most places, and in some places even taller.

Hastings moved briskly. Forster and Blaine followed along ducking thorny bush-limbs and trying to see where the trail would take them. When Hastings finally halted, faint starshine showed against a high, craggy rock-slope which arose abruptly from a small, secluded place where a number of trees grew amid tall grass hummocks. There was a tin-roofed, very old cabin back there. John leaned, gradually scowled, then said, 'Captain; how the hell did they get the lumber in here to make that house?'

Hastings turned, faintly smiling. 'They packed some of it on their backs, and the rest of it, the real heavy stuff, they brought in on pack horses.'

Blaine was impressed. 'Whoever he was who built it, sure wanted to be left alone.'

Forster's interest was not in the history of this secret place, it was in the possibility of Joseph Kramer being in the house. What made him have doubts was the fact that there was no road beyond the place, a mile and more back, where they had left their car, and there had been no other car back there. 'If he's here, how the hell did he get here?' Forster muttered, peering into the ghostly little secret place where the ancient, weathered old cabin stood. 'There was no car beside the road.'

Hastings was not too concerned about a car. There were dozens of brushy places along the road where someone who chose to conceal a car, could do so very easily. Hastings finally said, 'Well; *someone's* in there.'

John edged closer. 'I feel like an oldtime Indian about to attack a farmhouse, crouching out here in the night.'

Forster ignored this to address the captain. 'How do you know someone's in there, Ben?'

Instead of answering, Captain Hastings beckoned, and moved on down the trail another hundred yards, before stopping again. This time, he motioned for silence, and pointed to trampled grass near the cabin's only door, and from the trampled grass, to a pair of buckets with water in them, setting upon a bench nailed to the front of the cabin. Forster and Blaine understood. Hastings reached beneath his jacket, leaned back a little, and whispered. 'Remember, this guy's no push-over. If they cached a powerful short-wave set in there, you can damned well bet they cached some guns too.' Hastings, looking steadily at the cabin, shook his head irritably, then whispered again. 'This is the part I don't like. The law requires that you warn them before you jump them ... You fellows follow me to the edge of the clearing, then fan out into the underbrush, and when I call, you get set to shoot. My guess is that this son of a bitch isn't going to come out of there waving a dish-towel.'

They all went ahead as far as they dared, to the place where the underbrush had been cleared away, many years earlier, to allow a good view of the trail. Here, with the ghostly old cabin dead ahead, not more than about a hundred yards, Hastings gestured. Forster turned off into the brush on the right, and John Blaine, with a shorter distance to go, ducked from sight into the tall, spiny underbrush on the left.

Captain Hastings looked around for cover. There was none, so he went boldly ahead to the nearest sycamore tree, stepped behind it, palmed his snub-nosed service revolver, and called out.

'Kramer! This is Captain Hastings of the Los Angeles Police Department! I have a warrant for your arrest! Come outside!'

For ten seconds there was nothing but the quivering sound of a diminishing echo as Hastings's words went progressively up the backgrounding stone slope. Then all hell broke loose; someone inside the cabin cut loose with a sub-machinegun. Reg Forster dropped flat as the man in the cabin slowly stitched bullets from left to right, waist-high. He heard bullets strike the trees where

Hastings was flattened, with a solid, meaty sound.

CHAPTER EIGHTEEN

JOSEPH KRAMER, *FINI*

Only the man in the cabin had a dependable advantage, and as long as he could keep the initiative, he would be safe enough. No man in his right mind, holding a revolver in his hand and nothing else, could possibly feel fairly matched against an opponent with a sub-machinegun.

Reg Forster did not even raise up to look around until that stuttering gunfire coming from the cabin had ceased momentarily, and until after Captain Hastings had yelled out again to the cabin's occupant. Even then, as Forster lifted his head to peer through the undergrowth at the cabin, he thought they had done a needlessly chancy thing, coming up here, just the three of them, without any back-up.

After Ben Hastings's second call, the man in the cabin was silent for a while. Forster was made even more uneasy by this silence. If that were indeed Joseph Kramer in there, he might even prove the equal of three LAPD detectives. He certainly had had the kind of

165

training and experience that made a man not only a master of survival, but deadly dangerous and resourceful.

He did not answer any of Captain Hastings's calls. In fact, he did not make any sounds at all, from inside the cabin, except when he opened up with that sub-machinegun.

Forster, watching Hastings, who was pinned down at his sycamore tree, remembered the captain's call to the sheriff's sub-station in the Malibu vicinity, and wondered if there had been anything said about co-operation, up here. If there had been, Forster thought that right about now would be a nice time for a couple of carloads of deputy sheriffs to show up.

They didn't, the night continued deadly hushed after that first burst of gunfire, and Ben Hastings, behind his tree, was going to have to remain exactly where he was until either Doomsday, or the end of the man inside the cabin.

There was no sign of John Blaine, which there would not have been in any case, since he too was hidden in the underbrush. It occurred to Forster to try and flank the cabin, but he lay a long while thinking about it without making a move to implement the idea. A sub-machinegun was a terrible adversary. The man holding it did not have to be a good shot, in fact, it was a little like watering a lawn, a person simply had to keep the trigger depressed and swing the gun from side to side. If Forster tried to slip through the underbrush, and the man in the cabin heard nothing more ominous than underbrush rubbing against a moving object out there beyond the cabin, all he would have to do would be to spray bullets as he'd done before, and with no protection at all, except flimsy underbrush, Reg Forster would become a statistic.

Forster was not in any hurry to do anything. If this settled down to a waiting game, he and his companions had the advantage. At least, the man in the cabin could not escape, and if reinforcements arrived at all, they would be reinforcements for the police.

Hastings called again for the man in the cabin to come out, and as before, he got no answer. Forster, lying prone, studying the front of the cabin, thought he saw starshine reflected from shiny metal at the ridgepole of the cabin. He had not seen it before, probably, he told himself, because he had not looked up that high. But the thing was moving.

An aerial!

He crept forward a little to be sure. The metal rod stopped climbing while he watched. Forster looked towards Ben Hastings's tree, and beyond, over where John Blaine was. There was not much to see of Ben, and nothing at all to be seen of John.

Two thoughts crossed Forster's mind. The first thought was to the effect that the man inside the cabin was transmitting a wireless call for help. The second thought was to the effect that while the man inside the cabin concentrated on sending his May-Day call, he was not at the window with his machinegun.

Forster told himself he was being foolish to make the attempt, even as he rose to his knees and reached to part some underbrush for a better sighting of the cabin.

There was not a sound and, excepting Ben Hastings, who chose this moment to edge round his tree on Forster's side, neither was there any movement.

Ben was evidently seeking Forster; he was straining over in that direction. Forster moved a little, so Hastings could locate him, and at once the captain began gesturing. He too had seen the aerial pushed up for transmitting. He gestured with his stubby-nosed service revolver as though to shoot down the aerial, then he dolorously waggled his head. The idea, as Reg Forster interpreted it, was that using their service revolvers would not accomplish anything at this distance, against that aerial. Forster gestured that he understood, then disappeared back into his brush patch, working his way to the right, over in the direction of the small canyon's only low place, which was where the surplus spring water ran off, and promptly stuck a leg ankle deep into a smelly quagmire of black-grey soil, weeds, and brackish water.

He almost stuck the other leg, fighting to clear the one which was already in the mud. Afterwards, when he'd hoisted the leg out and had got to firmer footing, he stared in the direction of the cabin. That son of a bitch in there had put Forster to an awful lot of inconvenience lately.

He got to the north end of the cabin just as Captain Hastings tried to get some kind of response from the man in the cabin. As before, Hastings was wasting his breath.

Forster pressed to the cracked, warped old wood siding and waited until he heard what he thought was a voice speaking inside, then he moved very cautiously to the east corner of the cabin, and peeked around to see how far he was from the window. Not very far, perhaps twenty-five or thirty feet. He inched his way round until he was against the front of the cabin, and at about this time, the man inside moved, his footsteps heavy and echoing. Forster raised his revolver, felt his heartbeat falter, scarcely breathed, and when the footfalls came directly towards the window, Forster cocked his revolver. Across the rank grass in the near distance was the tree where Ben Hastings had been standing since the first exchange. Forster could even see up where John Blaine probably still was hiding. If any help came from those two for Reg Forster, he was perfectly willing to agree he would be in an equal amount of trouble as Kramer, because he and Kramer were very close together, now.

Forster heard the unmistakable sound of blued steel settling roughly against wood even before he saw the snout of Kramer's machinegun. Kramer himself did not lean into the starshine, but remained back in darkness. Forster eased his body around from the waist without moving his feet, staring hard at the exposed six or eight inches of gunbarrel. He had got himself into a position where he did not have much in the way of choices. He raised his thick left arm, paused a blurry second or two, then leaned ahead and clubbed downward at the same time. Pain like red-hot fire ran through his body as bone and muscle struck the exposed gunbarrel. He heard a man emit a guttural squawk as the gunbarrel was knocked aside and downward. Then Forster's whole body was in the window, his right hand with the cocked revolver swinging to bear on the thickly massive man back there in the gloom, whose reactions were surprisingly quick for a heavy, muscular person. Kramer's face showed for a second, then he lunged away from the window—and Forster squeezed the trigger. Impact half swung Kramer despite his squatty thickness. He threw out a hand to catch himself, missed the nearby little rickety table, and went down.

Forster yelled at him, half-deafened by the gunshot in those close quarters.

'Don't move!'

Kramer, one arm supporting the rest of his body on the floor, looked stunned, looked totally disbelieving, then he crumpled sidewards and Reg Forster, without turning, without taking his eyes off the injured man, called back.

'Ben! John! Get over here!'

He heard them coming through the rank grass but still did not turn. Blaine veered off and struck the door with his rather considerable heft. The door broke inward and John hesitated only for a fraction of a second, then jumped over where the machinegun lay, and kicked it savagely away.

Ben Hastings, beside Forster at the window, looked inside, then turned and walked to the broken door and entered. The last man inside the old cabin was Reg Forster.

There was not much in the cabin in the way of furnishings, three or four functional, battered old chairs, two tables, one large, one small—the very sophisticated short-wave radio was on the larger table—and there were three rickety old iron cots. One showed that it had been used recently; the covers and blankets were rumpled and flung back as though someone had jumped out of that bed in great haste.

Hastings pumped up the Coleman lantern, lit it, and under its intense white light, the three men got close to Kramer.

At the range Forster had fired, and also as a result of the calibre and kind of service revolver he had used, Joseph Kramer had a bad injury. He looked at the three detectives, and finally settled his stare upon Forster, to the exclusion of John Blaine, whom he also recognized, and Ben Hastings, whom he did not know at all.

Ben turned to speak to Blaine, to send him back to their parked car to call for medical aid, but Kramer spoke first. 'I didn't see how it could be you people. I didn't see how . . .'

Forster sank to one knee for a closer look at the gunshot wound. Even if John ran all the way back to their car radio, and even if the medics sent in their rescue helicopter, it would do no good. He raised his eyes, saw Kramer staring, and quietly said, 'It's pretty bad, Kramer.'

The wounded man evidently already knew this. He continued to stare at Forster when he spoke. 'How did you find this place?'

Instead of giving a direct answer, Forster said, 'The others are in custody. Oberhauser, his wife, the maid Peggy Bryan, and the new maid, Eilene Hamstead. On the East Coast, the FBI has by now made a roundup as well.'

Kramer was not to be diverted. 'How did you find me?'

Forster shrugged. Where Kramer was going, it would not make much difference what he knew. 'Oberhauser told us,' he said.

Kramer's retort was sanguine. 'I was supposed to kill him. The order came through last night. Someone in the Organization was a traitor.'

Forster could believe that, but he was certain the traitor was not Oberhauser. He thought, now, that it was quite possible they would never know, and that did not trouble him in the least. He leaned a little to make certain Kramer heard him, then said, 'You were the only one who could have killed the impersonator, Kramer. Neither of the women in the house could have got round your quarters and into the bushes where the assassin stood, without rousing you, and without leaving tracks. But you could do that—and you did.'

Kramer loosened against the floor and drifted his gaze to the pair of men standing over him. Then he drifted his gaze back to Forster's face again. 'It won't matter,' he murmured. 'Not now.' Then he said, 'I wirelessed for help.'

Forster nodded. 'If they try sending a trawler in close enough to land anyone, they'll be intercepted. The Coast Guard is on the alert all up and down the coast. So is the Civil Aeronautics Authority—with patrol aircraft. You were bottled up here, Kramer.'

The wounded man let out a ragged, long breath, and died.

Forster got stiffly back up to his feet, and

turned as a blinding light raked along the front of the cabin from back where the trail bordered the clearing. A bull-horn called out for anyone inside the cabin to come out. The caller identified himself as a member of the Los Angeles County Sheriff's Department.

Captain Hastings went to the door and called back, then led the way out into the blinding light. Six uniformed deputy sheriffs came forward, and just before they reached the three detectives, John Blaine made the same complaint he'd made before.

'What the hell are we doing, neck-deep in this spy-hunting business? Me, I prefer plain, commonplace homicide any day of the week. In this kind of a mess you don't have to figure things out, all you got to do is try not to get shot.'

Hastings agreed, then walked over to the leader of the deputies to converse, while Reg Forster glanced at the paling sky. It was almost dawn. He was tired, exhausted, dirty, and had a shoe full of foul mud. John was right, a decent, clear-cut case of murder was much better than this kind of mess, and he was heartily glad it was over. *Now*, the CIA could move in and have it all, including three corpses!

We hope you have enjoyed this Large Print book. Other Chivers Press or G.K. Hall & Co. Large Print books are available at your library or directly from the publishers.

For more information about current and forthcoming titles, please call or write, without obligation, to:

Chivers Press Limited
Windsor Bridge Road
Bath BA2 3AX
England
Tel. (01225) 335336

OR

G.K. Hall & Co.
P.O. Box 159
Thorndike, Maine 04986
USA
Tel. (800) 223-2336

All our Large Print titles are designed for easy reading, and all our books are made to last.